# Requiem

## A Kate Redman Mystery: Book 2

Celina Grace

# Chapter One

THE GIRL'S BODY LAY ON the riverbank, her arms
outflung. Her blonde hair lay in matted clumps,
shockingly pale against the muddy bank. Her face
was like a porcelain sculpture that had been broken
and glued back together: grey cracks were visible
under the white sheen of her dead skin. Her lips
were so blue they could have been traced in ink.
Purple half-moons pooled beneath the dark fan of
her eyelashes.

"So, what do you think?" asked Jay Redman.

His half-sister cocked her head to one side. "It's
very...powerful," she said cautiously. She reached a
finger out toward the scene, realising something.

"It's *not* a photograph, is it? Wow, it looks just
like one."

Jay Redman's painting technique was called
'hyperrealism'; it mimicked the precision of a
photograph, but the image was delineated in paint.
Kate looked at her little brother with a mixture of
affection and exasperation. She appreciated the

gesture, and God, Jay had real talent, but What on Earth made him think she'd want a picture of a dead girl hung above the fireplace? It was like looking at a crime scene photograph.

"It's great, isn't it?" said Jay. He adjusted the frame slightly, straightening it like a proud father pulling the shoulders of his son's first school blazer into shape. "Best thing I've done so far."

"Yes, indeed!" said Kate, trying to sound enthusiastic.

"It's for our end of year show. My tutor thinks it's great—he thinks it might even win the Bolton Prize."

"That's the top award, isn't it? That's brilliant, Jay. Why are you giving it to me?"

"I thought you'd like to have it for a while," said Jay, still staring proudly at the painting. "It's a housewarming present. On loan."

"Well, thank you."

"I'm calling it 'Ophelia Redux.'"

Kate felt another burst of affection towards her sibling. How wonderful it was to have someone in the family who knew Shakespeare, who had even *read* Shakespeare. It was clear why she and Jay got along so well, and it was something more than the fact that Kate had practically brought him up. There was no one else in the Redman family and its many offshoots who could talk about things other than reality television and the latest tabloid headlines.

Kate had pulled herself up by her bootstraps, and here was Jay, doing the same, even if the path he was taking was a different one to hers.

"It's great, Jay," she said, and her pride in her younger brother gave her tone a warmth which made her sound sincere. Jay beamed.

"I'm well proud of it," he said, reminding his sister that he did, in fact, have some way to go before he shook off his roots entirely. She gave herself a swift mental kick for being so judgemental.

"It's well good," she said, grinning. "Now, have you seen the rest of the house?"

"Can you show me after a drink?"

"Of course, sorry." Kate headed for the kitchen, still a little unfamiliar with the layout of her new house. She'd been here all of a week, and the rooms were still packed with boxes. "Tea?"

"Haven't you got anything stronger? We *are* supposed to be celebrating your move, you know, sis."

"Um..." Kate opened a few kitchen cupboards hopelessly. There was probably an ancient bottle of wine packed in one of the many cardboard boxes but where, exactly?

Jay rolled his eyes.

"Luckily for me, I know what you're like." He put his hand into his ragged green backpack and pulled out a bottle of champagne with a flourish. "See how good I am?"

"Jay, that's brilliant. How do you afford champagne on a student's budget?"

"Ah," said Jay. "Now there you have me."

"You didn't steal it?" gasped Kate, horrified.

"'*Course* not, sis, what do you take me for?" He leaned forward conspiratorially. "It's not real champagne. Just cheap fizz."

Kate smiled, relieved. "It'll do fine. As long as you don't mind drinking it out of mugs."

"Classy."

"I think you mean 'bohemian.'"

Kate sat on the sofa she'd brought from her old flat, and Jay took the new armchair she'd splashed out on when she moved. They clinked mugs and sipped. Kate found her gaze being drawn to the painting of the girl once more.

"Who's the model?" she asked. She looked at the mock-dead face, noting the fine bones under the unnatural pallor of her skin.

"My mate, Elodie."

There was a casualness in Jay's voice that didn't deceive Kate, especially with all her experience with reading what was unsaid.

"Girlfriend?"

Jay slugged back the rest of his champagne. "Nope, just a mate."

"Right," said Kate. She tipped a little bit more fizz in Jay's mug. "Is she on your course?"

Jay was in his second year at the Abbeyford School of Art and Drama, a further education college that specialised in the visual and dramatic arts. Kate had been thrilled when he'd decided to study there; her home town of Bournemouth was well over an hour's drive away from her new location, and while Jay had still lived at home, she'd not seen much of him.

"Nope. She's a musician, goes to Rawlwood."

Kate raised her eyebrows. "She must be good, then. They hardly accept anyone there, unless they're the new—um." She groped for a famous classical musician. "A new Stradivarius, or something."

"Eh?"

"I mean, it's really hard to get a place there."

Jay rolled his eyes. "Well, it probably helps that she's the Headmaster's daughter."

"Seriously?"

"Yep. But, actually, she *is* a talented musician, really good. She plays violin in this great band. Lorelei."

"Lorelei?"

"That's the band name. They play sort of folk rock. It's good—" Jay said, seeing Kate's unconvinced look. "Actually, there's a gig on tonight. I meant to tell you. Did you want to go?"

"Tonight?" asked Kate, doubtfully.

"Oh, come on," said Jay. "I know you normally need your plans signed off three weeks in advance before you commit to anything, but come on, sis, it'll do you good. You need to get out sometimes, you know. Start meeting people. Start joining in."

It was Kate's turn to roll her eyes. "I'm not a hermit, you know. I do have a social life."

"I'm not talking about hanging out with all your copper mates. That's not a social life—that's *work*. You need to get out and meet some normal people."

Kate laughed. "You're telling me police officers aren't normal people?"

Jay gave her a wry look and reached for the last of the champagne.

"No, sis, they are not. They are definitely not."

Kate twiddled her mug around in her hands. She'd planned a nice dinner for Jay's first visit to her new house, and then she'd assumed they'd sit in front of the fire and chat. That was what she felt like doing.

But his remark about her needing to know plans weeks in advance had stung a little. Was she really that inflexible? And when was the last time she'd actually *been* out, anyway? Somewhere that wasn't with her friend, and fellow officer, Mark Olbeck? She groped for a memory and realised that it must have been sometime in the summer: her friend Hannah's party. And now it was November. *All right, so I've had to organise a move in the meantime but honestly, I'm twenty eight, not eighty eight...*

She put the mug down and made up her mind.

"Sure, let's go. It'll be fun."

"Oh, cool, sis. You'll enjoy it. Elodie's great. You'll like her."

The faraway look in his eyes as he mentioned his

friend's name troubled Kate a little. She wondered whether Elodie knew how Jay felt about her. Well, she'd be able to see for herself later.

"Where's this gig?"

Jay tapped his phone's screen and began to scroll through his text messages.

"Arbuthon Green," he announced a moment later. "There's a pub there, the—"

"Black Horse," said Kate, sighing.

"You know it?"

"Yes." There had been several arrests there recently for drug dealing, but she wasn't going to mention that to Jay. So a night out at a dodgy pub listening to a student band? She was glad she hadn't drunk more than a mouthful of champagne; she'd be able to drive now and make a quick getaway if necessary.

"What about dinner?" she asked.

"Plenty of time for that later," said Jay. "I'll shout you some chips if you like."

"Perfect," said Kate ironically, standing up. "Come on." She nearly added 'let's get it over with,' but she didn't want to dampen Jay's obvious excitement. It would be nice to spend some time with her brother, anyway. She hadn't seen him for several months, after all.

"How's Mum?" she asked, once they were in the car and making their way to Arbuthon Green.

Jay looked at her in surprise.

"She's fine. Why? Haven't you seen her lately?"

Kate lifted one shoulder in a non-committal shrug.

"Not very lately. I've been so busy. With the move and everything."

Jay had his knees resting on the dashboard, and he was tapping them with his hands in response to some inner music.

"Mum's all right. She's got some new bloke on the go."

*Oh God.* Kate recalled some of the other 'blokes.' The fellow alcoholic, the married man, the other married man, the petty thief. She suppressed a sigh.

"What's he like?" she asked as they pulled into the car park of the Black Horse.

"All right, actually," said Jay, sounding surprised. "Seems fairly normal. Not like the others."

"Well, that's odd in itself," muttered Kate, almost under her breath. Then she dismissed her mother from her mind and concentrated on finding a parking space in the busy car park.

The pub was packed, standing room only. Jay and Kate battled their way through to the bar. Kate was already regretting her decision to come. She didn't want to stand up for two hours, shifting her weight from foot to aching foot, drinking warm orange juice and listening to some crappy amateur band. She felt a bit cross with Jay. Months since she'd seen him and now they weren't really going to have a chance to catch up at all...

She bought them both a drink after a long and frustrating wait at the bar. They battled back through the crowds to a spare square foot of space over by the back wall that was rather too near the toilets for Kate's liking.

The noise in the pub made it difficult to talk. There was a moment of silence between brother and sister as they sipped their drinks. Kate looked out at the heaving crowd. Lots of students, couples, noisy groups of young people. Denim, leather, piercings, spiky heels, band T-shirts. She looked down at her neat blue jeans and cashmere jumper in a tasteful shade of beige. Suddenly, she felt acutely out of place. Hot on the heels of that feeling, a much sharper surge of loneliness peaked. She felt totally apart from this raucous, happy crowd; it was as if she were observing them from afar, always on the outside looking in.

*That's what being a police officer does for you,* she thought, but she knew it wasn't just that.

She caught the eye of a man in the crowd who'd turned to look her way, as if attuned to her sudden emotional state. He looked familiar. She opened her mouth to greet him, looked closer, and shut it again. She didn't know him. Kate sipped her drink, cautiously looking back at the man, who'd turned to face the stage again. He still looked familiar. Kate mentally shrugged. She'd had this feeling before, and it usually meant she'd recognised someone she'd met in the course of her duties. Well, that was one way of putting it. Quite embarrassing, actually, running into someone you'd arrested.

She looked again at the man. He did actually have the faintly disreputable look of someone who might have rubbed up against the police at some point. His bone structure was good, you could even say he was raggedly handsome, but the overall impression was of good looks subjected to the major stressors of time, worry and hard living. He was staring at the stage, sipping a pint. Alone, like her.

No, not like her. She had Jay beside her, after all. She was aware that her brother had suddenly straightened up, quivering a little like a hunting dog spotting its quarry. There was an outbreak of noise from the expectant crowd: shouts, cheers, catcalls. Kate realised the band had made its entrance.

She spotted Elodie at once: blonde hair in an elfin crop which framed her fine-boned face. The girl had a violin in one hand, held casually but expertly against her hip, a bit like an experienced mother holds a baby. There was a male singer, hair a mass of knotty dreadlocks, nose ring glinting under the pub lights. A drummer and a guitarist, again both male, studenty, scruffy.

Elodie tucked the violin under her chin. The

singer counted his band members in, and they launched straight into their first number.

Three songs later, Kate was surprised to find that she was actually enjoying herself. The band, despite their scruffy appearance, were polished performers; they were well-rehearsed and talented and still had the charming enthusiasm of an amateur group. The songs were good, alternating between rollicking, stomping pop and quieter, more melodic ballads. Elodie came into her own during the slower pieces, her nimble fingers drawing plaintive, beautiful sounds from the strings of her violin. She played with great intensity, closing her eyes, seemingly lost in her own world of music.

Kate watched her face as she played, noting the high cheekbones and the sharp angle of her jaw. A beautiful girl, and beautiful in an uncommon way. There were plenty of pretty girls in the room, but Elodie had something else, some other quality that drew the eye. No wonder Jay was smitten.

The band finished their set with a rousing, raucous little number that had the crowd cheering and clapping. Elodie flourished her bow, laughing while she took a bow, and then the musicians all left the tiny stage.

Jay turned to Kate, raising his eyebrows. "Pretty good, huh?"

"They were excellent," agreed Kate.

"Let's go backstage, and you can meet her."

They battled their way through to the back of the pub. 'Backstage' was a bit of a misnomer—the band was crammed into a fetid little room just off the corridor, along from the toilets.

Kate was curious to see how Elodie greeted Jay. She was starting to wonder whether Jay actually knew her as well as he had implied, but she had to know him fairly well to agree to something like modelling for his painting, surely?

Her doubts were dispelled as Elodie caught sight of them. She shrieked and hurled herself at Jay, hugging him and landing a misdirected kiss on his ear.

"You came! What did you think? Were we good? Did you see me fuck up that last song? God!"

The questions came rapidly. Kate, ignored for now, could see the manic glitter in Elodie's eyes—the dilated pupils—now that she was close to the girl. Drugs? She really hoped no one would pull anything out in front of her. She'd *have* to arrest them, and then Jay would never forgive her.

Jay was laughing. He turned to her and gestured.

"Sis, this is Elodie. Elodie, this is my big sister, Kate."

"Hello," said Kate, reaching out to shake hands.

"Hi!" said Elodie. She pulled Kate forward into a hug—Kate squeaked in surprise—and kissed her cheek. The girl's body was thrumming with energy, her cheek warm and damp against Kate's.

"I thought you were really good—" began Kate.

"Oh thanks, you know, first nights are always tricky. Totally nerve-wracking."

"You haven't played here before?"

Elodie shook her head, her eyes sparkling. Kate suddenly saw what she must have looked like as a little girl: mischievous and cherubic at the same time, with blonde curls and chubby cheeks.

"Kate's seen the picture of you," said Jay. "You know, *the* picture. She loved it."

Elodie shrieked. "Damn you, Jay, that river bank was cold. And the *mud*...he made me lie in the mud for *hours*."

Even over the hubbub of the crowded room, Kate could hear her beautiful accent, each vowel and syllable falling neatly into place. It was easy to see how Elodie was the daughter of the head of Rawlwood College. Privately educated, loved and cherished, she must have had the best of everything. A girlhood so different to Kate's that it was difficult not to feel a surge of envy.

"So you're Jay's big sister?" asked Elodie. "He often talks about you."

Kate smiled. "All good, I hope." A clichéd response.

"What do you do?"

Kate glanced at Jay, wondering whether

to come clean. Being a police officer—and a detective especially—was like being a call girl or a gynaecologist. People were fascinated, and they wanted all the gory details, but at the same time, they were always a little uneasy in your presence.

"Um—"

She could see Jay shaking his head, a minute gesture easily passed between siblings.

It didn't matter anyway. She could see Elodie had lost interest in her answer; the girl's gaze was drawn up and over her shoulder. Kate watched the light die in Elodie's eyes, noticed the sudden dimming and shrinking of her personality. Elodie's smile faded. She muttered something like 'excuse me a minute' and pushed past Kate and Jay.

Kate turned round. The man she'd noticed earlier was standing in the doorway to the room, and Elodie was walking up to him, talking to him in a voice too low for Kate to make out their conversation. After a moment, they left the room together.

Kate frowned. Sensitive to atmosphere, she could feel the chill settling on the room. There was a sense that the party was over, that the best of the night was gone. She was suddenly aware of how tired she was.

She turned back to Jay.

"Do you want to make a move—" she began, stopping when she saw the bleak look on his face.

"What's wrong?"

Jay seemed to shake himself mentally.

"Nothing," he said, after a moment. She could see him forcing a smile. "I'm alright. Want a drink?"

Kate shook her head. "I'm bushed, Jay, and I've got to work tomorrow. Shall we head home?"

"I'm going to stay on for a bit."

"Really?"

Jay patted her arm. "S'alright, sis. Don't worry about me. You go on home and get some sleep."

"But how will you get back?"

"I'll get a cab. Don't worry."

Kate hunted in her bag before realising she didn't even have a spare key.

"I'll lock up, but just ring me on my mobile when you get back," she said. "I'll keep it by my bed."

"Yeah, cool." From Jay's distracted manner, she wasn't even sure he was listening. He was still staring at the empty doorway where Elodie and her male companion had been standing. Kate wavered for a moment, conscious of a faint nagging feeling of unease. Then she told herself not to worry. Jay was an adult, after all.

"See you later, then. I've made the spare bed up for you."

"Cheers, sis."

He hugged her goodbye, but she could tell his attention was still far away. *Oh well. Bedtime, Kate.*

She looked for Elodie as she walked to her car,

thinking she might see her outside the pub door, smoking cigarettes with the little crowd that had gathered there. There was no sign of her. Kate stood for a moment, her hand on the handle of the car door, wondering whether to look for her, to say goodbye and thank you. Then she dismissed the thought.

At that moment, all she wanted to do was get home and climb into her new bed.

# Chapter Two

WHEN KATE GOT TO THE office the next day, Olbeck was already there, hunched over his desk staring blearily and uncomprehendingly at the screen. He gave Kate the big, forced smile of a man pretending he didn't have a hangover.

"Good night?" asked Kate.

"Mmmph."

Kate said nothing, but she reached into her desk drawer and drew out a packet of paracetemol, which she threw across the desk.

"I'm *fine*," snapped Olbeck as the packet landed on his keyboard. "Just tired, that's all."

Kate said nothing. Olbeck relented.

"Sorry. Thanks."

Kate got them both a coffee and sat down again. She looked again at the text message from Jay, who hadn't come home last night. *Got a bed sis, wont be hm, c u later xx*. Sent at 4.13am. Whose bed? Elodie's or some random pick-up? Or simply a friend? She tried not to worry. *He's an adult*, she told herself, not for the first time.

She looked across at Olbeck, who was wincing and rubbing his temples. She wasn't going to worry about *him*, either. He was an adult too, although he currently wasn't acting much like one.

Olbeck had split up with his partner, Joe, several months ago. Having been the one to instigate the break-up, Olbeck had been making the most of his newly-found freedom. Night after night, he'd been out clubbing, partying, drinking and dancing. When he wasn't out living it up, he was working all hours, clocking up the overtime, constantly in the office. To Kate, it seemed very much like the actions of a man who was trying not to face up to something painful. However, having had her head bitten off more than once when she'd tried to broach the subject, she'd decided discretion was the better part of valour and was currently keeping her mouth shut.

She dismissed both Jay's and Olbeck's private lives from her mind, mentally squared her shoulders, and turned her attention to the massive amount of paperwork littering her desk while trying to ignore the long-suffering groans Olbeck kept making under his breath.

"What have we got today?"

Olbeck shoved a file across the desk.

"That domestic assault case is coming up."

"I thought Rav was doing that one?"

"He is, but—"

The phone rang. Olbeck picked it up.

"Olbeck here."

He said nothing else, but there was something in the change of his posture that made Kate sit up. She sat with pen poised, feeling her stomach tighten a little. It was a sixth sense, that's what it was; you knew when something big had happened. Olbeck wasn't saying much, just asking a series of blunt questions and scribbling down the answers. He said goodbye and put the phone down.

Kate put her pen down.

"What is it?"

Olbeck stood up, reaching for his car keys.

"Dead girl in the river. Patrol just called it in."

"Oh, no."

"Afraid so."

"Where?"

"Arbuthon Green."

Kate was reaching for her coat and looked up in surprise. "Seriously? I was there last night. Just last night."

"Should I arrest you?"

"Ha, bloody ha. Come on, you can tell me what you know in the car."

It was a twenty-minute drive to Arbuthon Green, and their route took them past the Black Horse, shut up now at 10.30am in the morning. The pavement outside was littered with cigarette stubs and empty bottles. Olbeck drove on through streets of terraced houses, their walls grey with pockmarked pebbledash and festooned with satellite dishes. Abbeyford was a reasonably affluent town, but every town has its poorer areas. Arbuthon Green was one of them.

The river was a winding oasis of beauty in the squalor. A footpath ran parallel with the water, and the banks were fringed with graceful willow trees, frondy branches dipping into the water. The banks were shallow, covered in patchy grass or thick mud. As Kate and Olbeck walked towards the little knot of people further up the footpath, they could see the pale shape of the body on the bank. No tent had yet been erected to screen the body from public view.

"Where's Scene of Crime?" Olbeck muttered, almost to himself, as they walked along.

Kate said nothing. As they got closer, she was aware of a sensation very much like shock that was beginning to set in. it was worse than shock: a sense of unreality, a feeling of dislocation. She could see the girl properly now; she was lying on her back, arms outflung. There was mud in her blonde hair, and her face was blue-lipped, ghastly pale.

"Oh my God."

Olbeck turned as Kate stopped walking.

"What's wrong?"

Kate was staring at the body. For a moment, she wondered whether she was still at home in bed dreaming.

"The body...it's the scene—"

"Kate, talk to me. You're not making sense."

Kate turned a pale face to Olbeck. "I know her. The girl. I met her last night."

Olbeck's face mirrored the shock on her own.

"You're kidding."

They'd reached the scene now. There were several uniformed officers, a shivering man in a wet tracksuit and Theo Marsh, one of Kate and Olbeck's colleagues.

Behind Theo, Olbeck saw the white vans of the Scene of Crime Officers draw up.

Theo raised a hand in greeting, and then frowned when he saw Kate's expression.

"What's up?"

Kate was breathing deeply, trying to get a hold of herself. She kept seeing the painting hanging even now on her living room wall: Elodie's mock-dead face, her blue lips. All brought to reality right in front of her. How was it possible? She brought a hand up to her face, pinching the bridge of her nose hard.

"First time, is it?" one of the uniforms asked in a bored and patronising manner.

"No, it bloody isn't," snapped Kate. She wheeled on one heel, not waiting to hear his response, and walked rapidly away along the riverbank. She took just ten steps before stopping, but it was enough to take her away from the body. The feeling of unreality receded slightly. She stood, back turned to the scene, watching the ripples on the surface of the river. Sticks and rubbish had drifted up against the muddy banks. Half a pumpkin floated by, one carved eye socket and several grinning teeth still evident, reminding Kate that Halloween had come and gone.

She heard Olbeck and Theo walk up behind her.

"Kate? You all right?"

She turned round. SOCO had already begun to cordon off the riverbank. The man in the wet tracksuit was being shepherded towards a waiting police car.

"I'm all right. It was just a shock."

"Mark says you know her," said Theo. He looked worried and young. This was a situation they'd discussed before, over drinks. *What if the victim was someone you knew? What would you do?*

Kate opened her mouth to tell them about the painting—and then shut it again.

"I met her last night for the first time. She's called Elodie. She's a musician, goes to Rawlwood College." She remembered what Jay had told her. "I think her father's the headmaster there."

Olbeck's eyebrows went up.

"God. If you're right, this is going to be..." He didn't need to elaborate to his colleagues.

"Are you sure it's her?" asked Theo. "I mean, if you've only met her once and with the water damage, and all..."

Kate was conscious of a sudden spurt of hope. How wonderful it would be if it *wasn't* Elodie. *Wonderful? Listen to yourself, Kate. You're talking about someone's daughter, someone's child.*

She dismissed her inner critic and walked up to the tape line, staring at the body. Once again, she was reminded of the painting. The posture, her face. Was it possible that the painting had actually caused her to misidentify the body because of the resemblance? Kate looked closer and her heart sank. It was definitely Elodie.

She walked back to the others, shaking her head.

"As far as I can see, it's her."

"Shit," said Theo. "We'd better tell Anderton as soon as he gets here."

"He's on his way now?" asked Olbeck.

Theo nodded. Kate watched the river slipping slowly past. She hadn't thought this far ahead yet. Anderton was the DCI for Abbeyford and surrounding areas; he was Kate's immediate boss. He would have to know about the picture. He would have to know everything. Kate remembered Jay sitting across from her on her new chair, tipping his mug full of champagne towards her, smiling.

CELINA GRACE

*Who's the model? My mate Elodie.*

"Kate?"

Kate realised she was standing with her eyes tightly shut. She gave herself a mental shake. *Get it together. You have no idea what's happened as yet, so stop panicking.*

"Here's Anderton," she said as she saw his car draw up, pleased her voice sounded so normal.

The three of them walked towards their DCI. Anderton had just returned from holiday—three weeks at his holiday home in the South of France, Olbeck had explained to Kate—and he was certainly tanned, his grey hair lightened by the sun. But he didn't look much like a man who'd enjoyed three weeks of relaxation. His brows were drawn down in a frown and there were dark circles under his eyes. *Probably doesn't want to be back at work, and who could blame him?* thought Kate as she returned his subdued greeting.

"Suicide, murder or accident?" said Anderton as they walked back towards the crime scene.

"We don't yet know, sir," said Kate. She pictured the painting hanging on her living room wall and heard her voice falter a little. When was she going to have to mention it?

"Well, any ideas at all? What have you people been doing all morning? Have I just been dragged down here to stand around like a spare part?"

Kate flinched under his tone. He could be

30

brusque, she knew that, but he was not normally so rude.

"A jogger discovered the body at about seven this morning," said Olbeck, hastily. "He thought someone was drowning, waded in and pulled them out, although obviously the girl was long dead by then."

"So the body was found in the river?"

"That's right, sir."

Kate grabbed Olbeck's arm. "Is that right? The body was pulled out of the river?"

"Yes," said Olbeck, looking down at her hand on his arm with a quizzical expression. "Didn't I say?"

"No, you bloody didn't!"

All three men were now looking at her strangely. Kate tried to pin a neutral expression on her face and tried not to show the waves of warm relief washing over her. The resemblance of the body on the riverbank to the picture on her wall was coincidental, that's all. Oh, wonderful relief. For a moment, she felt dizzy with it.

"Something wrong, Kate?" Anderton spoke in a voice that implied she had to tell him.

Kate struggled and managed to subdue her euphoria. "Sorry sir, nothing wrong. I just hadn't been informed of all the facts, that's all." Olbeck shot her a hurt look, which she ignored. "I wasn't aware that this wasn't the original crime scene."

Anderton exhaled in disgust.

"You lot are not impressing me this morning. Theo, tell me something useful, for Christ's sake."

"Yes, sir." Theo almost stood to attention. "As Mark said, the body was discovered by a jogger, Mike Deedham, this morning at about seven am. He often runs along this path, according to him. He said he saw something in the water—in fact, he said he saw 'someone' in the water—and thought they were drowning, plunged in, dragged them out onto the river bank and then realised they were, well, dead already."

"Humph." Anderton looked over at the police car where the man in the wet tracksuit had been taken. "That's *his* story. We'll have to take a much more detailed statement. Anything else? Do we know who the victim is yet?"

Olbeck nudged Kate's arm and she shot him an annoyed look. Anderton intercepted it. "Kate Redman, what is the matter with you this morning? Do you know who the victim is, or not?"

Kate spoke. "Yes sir. She's a young student called Elodie, I'm not sure of her last name." Olbeck nudged her again. "For fuck's sake, Mark! Let me finish. She's a musician, a student at Rawlwood College."

Anderton studied her face.

"And how do you know all of this?"

Jay's face swam in front of her eyes. Kate swallowed. "Because I met her last night, sir."

Anderton's grey eyes regarded her steadily.

"Is that so?" he said. "Well, you'd better tell me all about it."

# Chapter Three

ELODIE DUNCAN LIVED—HAD LIVED—WITH HER parents in a house on the grounds of Rawlwood College. The house was named Rawlwood Cottage, which was something of a misnomer, as Kate and Olbeck discovered. They drove up the long and winding gravel driveway to the impressive Victorian building that stood in a clearing of evergreen and deciduous trees. Hidden from view from the main road behind a bank of trees, the house was very large, the gables and window frames painted black, original stained glass in the front door. There were two cars parked neatly side-by-side in front of the house: a dark purple Volvo and a newer model Beetle in silver.

"Did Elodie have a car?" asked Mark as they made their way to the front door.

"I don't know—" Kate was unable to say more, as the door opened before she'd even raised a hand to the doorbell. The man who had opened it was in his late fifties: tall, rather handsome and dressed in a well-cut tweed jacket. There was something slightly wrong with his appearance, something so subtle that Kate could hardly put her finger on what it was. Then she realised it was his tie. It was a colour that clashed slightly with the tweed of his suit and the knot was tied badly, obviously in haste.

"May I help you?"

"Mr Duncan? Thomas Duncan?"

"Yes? What's the matter?"

Olbeck and Kate showed their warrant cards. "We're police officers, sir. May we come in for a moment?"

Mr Duncan remained where he was for a moment, one hand on the half-open door. He closed his eyes.

"What's happened?" he said, in a voice almost too faint to be heard.

"May we come in, Mr Duncan?" Kate wasn't going to do this on the doorstep, whether or not the house was isolated.

The headmaster opened his eyes.

"Yes, of course," he said. He seemed to pull himself together a little. "I'm sorry. Come through..."

They followed him through the hallway and into a sitting room to the left. A woman was perched there on the very edge of the sofa, clasping her hands together. She was blonde, petite: an older, faded copy of Elodie.

"This is my wife, Genevieve Duncan," said Thomas Duncan. Kate had the impression that the two of them had been sitting there all night, waiting. Were they waiting for their daughter, who was never coming home? She took a deep breath. This was the worst part of her job, the very worst. It never got any easier.

"Mrs Duncan, Mr Duncan, I'm very sorry to have to tell you that I have some very bad news." Say it quick, don't ever drag it out. People at this point know the worst has happened, there was never any need to prolong the agony. "This morning, we found the body of a girl which we believe to be your daughter Elodie. I'm so sorry—"

Mrs Duncan burst out in screams, in full-blown hysteria: piercing yells, tears streaming down her pale cheeks. Mr Duncan knelt by her, his face grey. She threw her hands over her face, writhing and kicking like a toddler having a tantrum.

Kate looked at Olbeck. He met her eyes, but there was no need to say anything. There was nothing they could do but wait.

After a seemingly endless stretch of time, Mrs Duncan's sobs tapered off into gasping breaths. She lay back against the cushions of the sofa, still hiding her face. Kate had seen that impulse in people before: the wish to shut out the knowledge, an attempt to physically block off the horror.

Mr Duncan sat by her, his hands dangling between his knees.

"I'm so very sorry," Kate said, quietly. "This must

have been a terrible shock to you. I'm afraid I will need one of you to come with us to identify her."

She looked directly at the headmaster. "Mr Duncan, are you able to do that?"

Mr Duncan got up from the sofa, moving like a man twenty years older than himself.

"Me? I don't know if I could bear it." He looked at his wife, helplessly. "No, I must, I can see that I must."

"Is there someone who could stay with your wife to give her some support? DS Olbeck will stay here as well, but perhaps a friend..."

"I don't know, I—"

"I don't want anyone," said Mrs Duncan, in a voice ragged with tears.

Kate nodded slightly at Olbeck. She stood back slightly to let Mr Duncan make his slow and shaky way past her to the hallway.


At the mortuary, he stood in silence, with Kate beside him, regarding Elodie's body. His gaze lingered on her pale face. The dead never look as though they are sleeping, not when looked at properly. Something—call it the soul, the spark of life—something indefinable has gone. The dead look truly dead.

Kate thought of her first glimpse of Elodie; the girl's impish grin and vivid personality shining out from the stage. And now this, a whole person reduced to a hollow shell, lying on a cold metal table. She felt tears come to her eyes.

As if he could sense her pain, Mr Duncan began to speak, falteringly, almost as if he were talking to himself.

"She was always special. She had a glow about her, something special—everyone around her could feel it. She was eight years old when I met her, and I could see it then. Oh yes," he interjected as Kate made some kind of noise in response, "I'm her stepfather. But that never mattered. She always felt like mine, just as if she were my real daughter. Yes, mine..."

His voice faded away. Kate sensed a huge tidal wave of emotion, held back by the flimsiest of barriers.

"Always special," said Mr Duncan, his voice shaking. The dam broke. He put his hands up to his face, tears running down between his fingers. Kate put a hand on his trembling arm.

"It shouldn't be like this!" he cried, and then his words were lost in a torrent of sobs. Kate, feeling her uselessness, kept a steadying hand on him, muttering the usual soothing words.

Later, after driving Mr Duncan home, Kate and Olbeck conferred briefly with the family liaison officer now stationed at the house. Mrs Duncan was sat at the kitchen table, staring out at the garden, a cup of tea untouched before her. Kate wondered whether to interview the parents now or whether to wait until the first shock had worn off a little. She decided on the latter.

"God," said Olbeck as they got into the car. He leant his head against the back of the car seat and closed his eyes. "That was a bad one."

"Especially on a hangover," said Kate unsympathetically.

"You have no idea." He sat up again, rubbing his temples. "Actually, I need a drink."

"No, you don't."

"I do. A bloody big one."

"I'll buy you one."

Olbeck looked at her in surprise. "You will?"

"A giant coffee," said Kate, smiling a little. "Perhaps even a muffin to go with it."

"Huh." Olbeck slumped again. "We'd better get back, anyway."


Later that afternoon, Kate, Olbeck and Anderton returned to Rawlwood Cottage. Normally, the three of them would use the time in the car to discuss the case, bring forward points they thought worthy of discussion, make suggestions about where to go next. Today, though, they sat in silence, all three of them busy with their own thoughts. Kate stared out of the window as they turned into the driveway, past the crumbling stone gateposts and through the banks of trees still clothed in their autumn leaves. She was thinking about the painting. When was she going to mention it? *Was* she going to mention it? Wasn't it just a coincidence that the crime scene so closely resembled the picture? *The body was found in the river*, she told herself, trying to ignore that small voice inside that told her that it could still be important.

"Kate! Wake up. We're here."

Anderton's voice made her jump. She gave herself a mental shake and got out of the car, smoothing back her hair and trying to get herself back into the right state of mind for this interview.

The Duncans were sitting in the living room. Mrs Duncan hunched into an arm chair; her husband perched on the edge of the sofa. The family liaison officer, a PC called Mandy, stood up as the other officers came into the room. Anderton introduced himself and his team.

"I'll make us all some tea," said Mandy. Kate smiled at her as she walked past to the kitchen. Briefly she wondered how many millions of cups of tea the liaison officers made in the course of their careers.

Anderton began with a few words of sympathy. Mrs Duncan kept her eyes on the arm of her chair, her fingers rubbing and picking at the fabric.

"I don't know what we can tell you," said Mr Duncan. "We don't know any more than you do. Elodie went out last night—she was in a band and they were playing at a pub, The Black Horse. I don't know what happened."

"Did you expect Elodie to come home last night?"

"She was meant to."

Anderton leant forward a little.

"Does that mean that you did expect her home, or not?"

The Duncans exchanged a glance. Then Mr Duncan said, reluctantly, "We did expect her home but...we weren't sure whether she would be or not."

Mrs Duncan gripped the edge of the seat arm, the bones of her fingers showing bluish-white through the skin of her hands.

"She's been so odd recently..." she began falteringly, and then obviously realised the mistake in her use of the present tense. Tears began to stream down her cheeks, but she kept speaking. "She was so secretive, moody—we used to get so upset with one another, I don't know...I didn't know what to do."

Anderton looked at Kate, and she responded to his unseen cue, taking up the baton.

"Were you worried when Elodie didn't come home, Mrs Duncan? Had she done this before—stay out all night without letting you know when she'd be home?"

Mrs Duncan nodded.

"The past few months have been particularly bad. She was so argumentative. Nothing her father or I could do was right. Ever since her eighteenth birthday, she's just run wild." She stopped abruptly and put her face in her hands.

Kate turned to Mr Duncan, who was staring blankly at the carpet.

"Did Elodie have a boyfriend?"

"No."

He said it harshly, almost angrily. Then he seemed to recollect himself. "I'm sorry. She did have a boyfriend for a few months, but that didn't last long. There wasn't anyone else."

Kate glanced at Olbeck, who looked back at her expressively. How much did these parents actually know of their daughter? She wouldn't have been the first teenager to hide an unsuitable boyfriend from their knowledge.

"We'll need the name of Elodie's ex-boyfriend, please, and also the names of her friends, the people she used to spend a lot of time with."

Neither of the Duncans spoke for a moment. Then Mrs Duncan, fingers unconsciously pulling at the fabric of the chair on which she sat, said, "His name was Reuben, Reuben Farraday."

"Is he a pupil at Rawlwood College?"

"He is not," said Mr Duncan. "He and Elodie met at a concert. I'm afraid I have no knowledge of where he is now." He and his wife exchanged another look. "I'm afraid I didn't much approve of him."

"Was that why they split up?"

"I don't know." His tone indicated that he would prefer not to continue talking about this particular subject, which normally would mean that Kate and the team would start to push harder. But these parents had just lost their daughter and, after a tiny shake of the head from Anderton, Kate switched subjects.

"You mentioned Elodie's behaviour had changed over the past couple of months, Mrs Duncan. Did you know why that was?"

Mrs Duncan shook her head. "Every time I tried to talk to Elodie about how badly she was behaving, she just got worse. Eventually, I just didn't dare to bring it up anymore."

"How was she behaving badly?"

Mrs Duncan wiped her face. "I thought I'd already said. She was rude, moody. Such hard work to be around. She didn't want to do anything with me, with Tom, with anyone."

"So she didn't go out much?"

An incredulous look. "She went out *all the time*. She was never at home. But she would never say who she was going out with."

"Did she ever bring any friends home?"

"Amy came over sometimes." Mrs Duncan sniffed. "She's known her for years. She's a nice girl."

"Amy is Elodie's best friend? What's her surname?"

"Peters." Mrs Duncan hesitated, pulling again at

the arm of the chair. "She hasn't been round for a while. I think Elodie and she had an argument."

"An argument? What about, Mrs Peters?"

Mrs Duncan shook her head.

"I don't know. I don't know anything."

There was a moment's silence. Kate thought back through the conversation, making a mental list of the words used by Elodie's mother. *Moody, difficult, secretive...* She recalled the manic glitter she'd seen in Elodie's eyes, and her heart sank a little. As if reading her thoughts, Mr Duncan asked in an almost inaudible voice, "How did she die?"

Mrs Duncan winced as if he had shouted. Anderton shook his head slowly.

"We don't yet know, I'm afraid. The post-mortem will tell us more."

Mr Duncan opened his mouth as if to ask another question and then shut it again. There was a lengthy moment of silence in the room. Kate caught sight of a photograph of a younger Elodie on the mantelpiece, framed in silver. She had an impish grin on her face and was staring out of the frame, pointed chin lifted. She looked as though she were laughing at them all.

# Chapter Four

KATE HAD ATTENDED MANY POST-MORTEMS in the course of her career, but they had yet to become commonplace. She steadied herself with a deep breath. She always felt something like awe at the magnitude of death—how a whole, remarkable person could be reduced down to a waxen reproduction of themselves. The pathologist performing the autopsy was someone Kate hadn't met before, a young man called Stanton. She had hoped it would be Doctor Telling, who she rather liked for being quiet and gentle and skilled at her job, but she was apparently on holiday for three weeks. Kate's mind conjured up a rather bizarre mental picture of the gaunt, pale doctor sunning herself on a beach somewhere, still dressed in her pathologist's scrubs. She dismissed the thought, as it was provoking an inappropriate grin, and brought herself back to the task in hand.

Anderton had cried off, citing a meeting, but Olbeck had met her at the coroner's offices, turning up looking rather better than he had done yesterday. Presumably he'd not been out partying to the early hours the night before. Kate could understand his decision to stay in; she could think of few things worse than having to observe an autopsy with a raging hangover. She said as much to Olbeck.

"What would you know about it?" he said, rather grumpily. "You never *get* hangovers. You hardly bloody drink."

"I can still imagine it."

"Well, anyway. Let's get on with it."

Dr Stanton had a rather brusque manner, tersely commenting as he performed the various tasks that would untangle the mystery of Elodie's death.

"Are there any indications of suicide?" asked Olbeck, who'd disappeared halfway through the operation to answer a text message, rather to Kate's annoyance.

"Most definitely not," said Stanton. He turned away from the table, leaning back against the instrument bench against the wall. "There's no water in the lungs, which is always a good indication."

"Ah."

"And more pertinently than that, the hyoid bone is fractured."

Kate knew the significance of that. "So she was strangled?"

Doctor Stanton looked at her appraisingly and then smiled rather flirtatiously.

"The indications are there. Bruises on the neck as well."

"Right."

"I don't believe we've met before, have we? This will all be in my report, by the way. I'm happy to talk you through it—perhaps over coffee afterwards?"

Olbeck was grinning. Kate sighed inwardly. Flirting was one thing, but doing it over the body of a dead girl was distasteful in the extreme.

"That's fine, thank you. I can read it later."

Stanton shrugged. "There's one thing you should know."

"Which is?"

"She was pregnant."

Kate felt the familiar little tremor inside her, as if a tiny foot had swung against her lower belly. When would she stop feeling that?

She cleared her throat. "How pregnant?"

"Not very. First trimester. About ten weeks, I'd estimate."

Olbeck had stopped smiling. "That's something her parents didn't know."

"Or they didn't tell us." Kate tried to run a hand through her hair, knowing it was pure displacement activity, before realising it was tied back tightly. "We'll need to talk to them again anyway." She remembered something else. "What about drugs? Any indications?"

Stanton had begun to peel off his gloves.

"You'll have to wait for the tox tests. I should have the results within a week. There was plenty of alcohol and not much food in her stomach."

So Elodie had been drinking despite her pregnancy. Had she even known she *was* pregnant? Who was the father? If Elodie had known she was pregnant, had she told anyone else? Looking down at the body, shrouded now in dull green cotton, Kate felt tired. So many questions... It was hard to know where to begin.

"Do you know the time of death?" asked Olbeck.

Stanton was rinsing his hands under the tap. He pulled a handful of blue paper towels from the dispenser on the wall, dried his hands and threw the crumpled up ball of paper into a wastebin next to him.

"It's hard to say exactly, as well you know. But— like I say in my report—you can narrow it down to between about 3am and 5.30am the night before last."

"He fancied you," said Olbeck, when they were back in the car.

"No, he didn't."

"Yes, he did. It was obvious. You were definitely in there."

Kate snorted. "Even if I was, I'm not going out with a *pathologist*, for God's sake. Can you imagine going to bed with one, for a start? You'd always be wondering where their hands had been. Ugh."

Olbeck chuckled. "Perfect partner for a necrophiliac."

"Well, quite." Kate flicked the indicator on to turn left. "As for me, it's thanks but no thanks."

"All right, all right. I get the message." Olbeck checked his phone and made a satisfied noise.

Kate glanced over. "What's up?"

"Nothing," he said, smugly.

Kate sighed. "Don't tell me. Your hot date for tonight."

"Got it in one."

"You have more hot dates than I have hot dinners," grumbled Kate. "And what was with the texting during the PM? That's not professional, Mark."

"Oh, leave it out, Kate. It could have been work-related for all you know."

"Well, was it?"

Olbeck was silent for a moment. "It might have been."

"*Was* it?"

"No." He grinned a little sheepishly. "But come on, it was only a minute. Besides, don't tell me you've never done anything unprofessional at work." He laughed a little. "Wait, what am I saying? This is DS Redman we're talking about."

Kate said nothing. She knew he was just teasing

her, but his words had brought the painting sharply back to the forefront of her mind. Was she going to mention it? Should she? *Of course you should, and you know it*, a little voice whispered. Hard on the heels of that thought came the question, *Does Jay know yet? Am I going to have to tell him?* Kate shivered inwardly, already dreading the moment.

# Chapter Five

THE CRIME SCENE PHOTOGRAPHS WERE already pinned up to the whiteboards when Kate entered the office the next day. The night before, she'd taken the picture down and put it away in an upstairs cupboard. Then she'd locked the cupboard door. She'd tried to call Jay, but the call had gone straight to his voicemail, so she'd hung up without leaving a message. Cowardly but... Kate's train of thought was derailed as Anderton crashed through the door.

"Morning team, morning team." He strode up to the whiteboards and pinned up another photograph beside the one of Elodie's body. This new picture made a cruel contrast: it was a recently taken shot, professionally posed, obviously a school picture. Elodie in the dark blue and silver uniform of Rawlwood College, shoulders held back, pointed chin lifted, blonde crop neatly brushed. She looked younger, somehow, than she had when Kate met her. Perhaps it was the uniform. Perhaps it was the expression on her face, eyes big and dark, a hint of anxiety in her gaze.

Anderton seemed to have recovered his mood and was back to his normal ebullient self. The rest of the team took up their usual positions, angled to keep their chief in sight as he paced up and down the room.

"Elodie Duncan," said Anderton. "Our victim. Eighteen years old, a pupil at Rawlwood College, daughter of the College's headmaster."

"Stepdaughter," said Olbeck.

"Yes, that's right. Stepdaughter." He stopped pacing for a moment, clutching his hair with one hand. "Her body was found at 7.06am two days ago by a jogger on the footpath that runs along the river by Arbuthon Green. Cause of death now confirmed as manual strangulation. Kate!" Kate jumped. "Wake up. Anything pertinent from the PM?"

Kate took a deep breath.

"She was pregnant. Early stages, about ten weeks."

"Aha," said Anderton. He turned and put a finger out, touching the school picture of Elodie almost tenderly. "That's interesting. Do her parents know, I wonder?"

"That's what we thought," said Olbeck. Kate hadn't had a chance to talk to him yet. She looked over at him, noting with irritation mixed with concern that he looked even rougher than he had done the other day. What was the matter with him? He was acting like a teenager. Immediately her thoughts snapped back to Jay, and by association, the painting. *You've got to do something or stop thinking about it,* she told herself. *This is how madness starts.*

Anderton was still talking.

"We've spoken to Elodie's parents. They're not telling us much at the moment, but it seems our girl's been moody, difficult, argumentative. Out of control, in her parents' eyes. Now this may be nothing more than the usual teenage rebellion, but it may not be. I want all her friends interviewed. Let's see what they can tell us. I've already cleared it with her father that we can use a room at the College for as long as we need for interviews. We need to find this ex-boyfriend of hers too."

Jerry raised his hand.

"What about the bloke who found the body?"

"Yes, indeed. I want to hear his story myself. Told us he thought he saw someone drowning, jumped in to try and save them, pulled out the body. Now he may be telling the truth, or it may be his way of covering up something more sinister. *Kate.*"

Kate came back to reality with a start. "What, sir?"

"Did you have a late night, or something? Wake up. What's the jogger's name?"

Kate groped for a moment and then thankfully her memory returned.

"His name's Michael Deedham."

"Deedham, right. We need to interview him again. Mark, Kate, come with me after this meeting, and we'll knock that off to start with." Anderton reached the wall, turned sharply on his heel and began pacing back the other way. "Right, what else?"

Kate thought it was time she made a real contribution. "Mark and I will start interviewing her friends. They may know a lot more about Elodie's life than her parents do."

"Good point." Anderton shot her a piercing glance. "Didn't your brother know her?"

Kate felt her heart rate begin to speed up a little. She could see the painting in her mind's eye: the river bank, the mud, Elodie's dead face. She swallowed.

"That's right." She paused for a second. "I'm not sure how well he *actually* knows her though."

"Well, it'll do for a start. What about girlfriends? Her mother mentioned her best friend, whose name escapes me at the moment. Anyone?"

Olbeck shifted his position, leaning against one of the tables.

"Amy Peters," he said, looking down at his notes. "We'll track her down."

"The ex-boyfriend, too," said Kate. "Reuben Farraday."

"Her teachers," said Theo.

"Good, good. All this needs to be followed up. Jane, get onto the CCTV from that stretch of the river. In fact, from anywhere near the last place she was seen alive, which was the Black Horse."

Jane's red curls bounced as she nodded.

Anderton finally came to a halt.

"Right, that'll do to go with. Anyone else got anything to say?"

"You haven't mentioned the pregnancy, sir," said Kate. "Do we mention it in our interviews?"

"Christ, yes. How did I forget that?" Nobody answered him, although there were a few disconcerted glances exchanged. It was unusual for Anderton to admit to a mistake and even more unusual for him to make one. "So, Elodie Duncan was...what was it? Ten weeks pregnant when she died. Now, the question is, does this have any bearing on her death or is it coincidence? Why didn't her parents mention it? Do they even know?" He ran both hands through his hair and dropped them to his side. "Yes, mention it. Well, see how the conversation is going and use your discretion. I want to know whether it's important or not. Right, team, you've got your orders. Start digging. Get—"

"The evidence," they all chorused, finishing his sentence. Anderton grinned.

"That's right. Okay, Kate, Mark—let's go."

The jogger who'd reported the discovery of the body, Michael Deedham, lived in a red-brick Edwardian villa in Charlock, the neighbouring suburb to Arbuthon Green. Both Charlock and Deedham's house were a great deal more prosperous and respectable-looking than the poky terraces and down-at-heel flats that made up most of Arbuthon Green. Deedham was an athletic-looking man of around forty, balding and muscular. He had looked more at home in the damp tracksuit he'd been wearing when Kate and Olbeck had seen him at the crime scene than he did in the well-cut suit he was wearing when he opened the door to them. Although they'd rung ahead to announce their visit, he still looked a little disconcerted at their appearance.

They were ushered into a sitting room at the front of the house that was furnished with a battered leather Chesterfield and a rather jarringly modern armchair. Children's plastic toys and a jumble of wooden train set pieces were scattered over the worn Persian rug.

"Sorry about the mess," said Deedham, kicking a battered plastic doll and a few toy cars over to the skirting board. "Two kids under three, what can you do?" He didn't seem to require an answer. "What can I do for you?"

He had a brisk manner which Kate associated with teaching for a living. She asked him what he did for a job.

"I'm a management consultant," he said. "With Seddons Hargrove." Kate nodded to give the impression that she actually knew what a management consultant was. What was it exactly that they did?

Olbeck and Anderton had seated themselves on the Chesterfield, leaving Kate to choose the modern chair. She perched somewhat gingerly on its edge.

"We'd just like to talk to you again about the events of the day before yesterday," began Anderton. "Take us through the timeline, so to speak."

Deedham had taken the only other chair in the room, a rickety wooden one. He frowned.

"I've already given a statement."

"I know, sir," said Anderton smoothly. "This is very much standard procedure. There's nothing to worry about."

"I'm not worried. I just don't understand why I have to go through it all again. It was a pretty distressing experience."

"It must have been. So, you were on your usual morning run?"

Deedham sighed and gave in.

"That's right. I run every morning, sometimes in the evenings as well. I'm training for the London marathon, and I have to put in the hours, because I'm deskbound for the rest of the day. Anyway, I was doing the usual route, along the path by the river, and I spotted something white in the water."

CELINA GRACE

"Could you see it was a person?"

"Not at first—I just saw this large, white thing in the river, then this hand came up." He raised his own arm to demonstrate. "And I think, my God, it's someone drowning. So of course I kicked off my trainers and leapt right on in."

"You didn't realise that the girl was already dead?"

Deedham looked annoyed.

"No, I didn't. Not until I got her out onto the bank anyway. Look, what was I supposed to have done, leave her to drown?" He pulled himself up. "I mean, I thought she was drowning. Jesus Christ, next time I won't bother."

"All right, Mr Deedham. We know you were trying to do the right thing. We just have to have everything absolutely straightened out, to make sure we've got everything down correctly."

Deedham ran a finger around his collar, as if it had suddenly become too tight.

"I tried mouth to mouth," he said in a clipped tone. "Now you're probably going to tell me I was wrong to do that as well."

Kate and Olbeck exchanged glances.

"Of course not, Mr Deedham," said Kate, taking up the conversation. "That was very public-spirited of you. I suppose even though you knew she was dead, you thought there might be a chance to bring her back to life?"

58

Deedham nodded. All of a sudden his eyes filled with tears.

After a moment, he said with a catch in his voice, "I didn't try for long. I could see it wasn't going to work. She was cold as anything, lifeless—like a doll, really..."

He trailed off into silence. Anderton let it spool out for a couple of seconds and then asked, "Did you know Elodie Duncan, Mr Deedham?"

Deedham stared.

"*Know* her? What, aside from pulling her out of the river?"

"Yes. Did you know her in—life, shall we say?"

Deedham was still staring. "No. I'd never seen her before in my life."

"Are you sure?"

"Yes, of course. Why?" Nobody answered him. "I promise you I'd never clapped eyes on her before, poor girl."

"You know that she was the daughter of the Headmaster, Thomas Duncan, at Rawlwood College?"

"Was she?" Deedham rubbed his balding head. "No, I didn't know that."

"Have you any connection to the College?"

Deedham got up out of his chair and stood behind it, gripping the back of it.

"No, I haven't got any *connection* to the College.

I don't understand all these questions. What are you implying?"

"It's standard procedure, sir," said Kate, knowing that Anderton liked her to step in at these moments. *It's something about the softer voice, Kate,* he'd said when they'd talked about it. She'd called him an utter sexist, but it did seem to work when a suspect was becoming aggressive. "I'm sorry if you find this intrusive, but you have to understand that in a murder case, we're operating from a standpoint of complete ignorance. We have to ask a lot of questions to try and see where we're going."

Deedham looked at her. She smiled, and he looked a little mollified.

"You're being very helpful, sir," Kate added. "We are very grateful. As I'm sure Elodie's parents are for what you tried to do for their daughter."

"Okay," said Deedham, shortly. He sat down again, pulling at his jacket sleeves. "I'm being totally honest with you. I'd never seen her before or heard of her, and I had no idea she was anything to do with whatever it was College. That's all."

There was the sound of the front door banging open and then the squeal of young children's voices out in the hallway. A few seconds later, the doorway opened and a yelling toddler barrelled into the room. The little boy came to a screeching halt as he realised there were three strange adults in the room.

"It's all right, Harry, it's all right," said Deedham, picking his son up. The boy hid his face in his father's broad chest. A woman put her head around the door.

"Oh, sorry," she said, looking puzzled.

"It's the police," said Deedham. His wife's face clouded. "They want to know whether I knew Elodie Duncan."

"Who?"

Deedham looked at the police as if to say 'you see?'

"That poor girl I pulled out of the river."

"Knew her?" His wife came fully into the room. She was a small woman, neat and pretty, with a chin-length bob haircut. She had a baby settled on her hip, a girl of about eight months who looked at the police officers with round eyes and began sucking her small thumb.

"Of course he didn't know her," said Mrs Deedham. "He'd never seen her before in his life."

The little boy in Deedham's arms began to struggle. His father put him down on the floor, and he immediately ran over to a box of toys in the corner of the room and began throwing them aside, clearly searching for a particularly loved one. The officers exchanged glances. The time for questioning was obviously at an end. They got to their feet.

CELINA GRACE

"So what do you think?" asked Olbeck as they drove back to the station.

Anderton was driving. Technically, his work status warranted a driver, but Kate had noticed that he always preferred to drive himself. He liked to be in control.

He shrugged and made an indeterminate noise. "I don't know. There's nothing about his statement that doesn't add up but...I don't know."

"I know what you mean," said Kate. "He's very defensive."

"It's not so much that." He slowed the car for a T-junction, glancing at her in the rear view mirror. "There's something about him I don't like. I can't put my finger on it. It may be important—then again, it may not."

"Should we talk to his wife?" asked Kate. "See if she says anything that, well, doesn't quite tally?"

Anderton pondered. "Yes. But it's lower priority at the moment than the other interviews. We start at Rawlwood College tomorrow, nine sharp." They were approaching the station. He caught her eye again. "You talked to your brother yet?"

"Not yet, sir, sorry," said Kate, adequately disguising the drop of her stomach. "I haven't been able to get hold of him. I'll try again once I'm back at my desk."

# Chapter Six

KATE CALLED IT A NIGHT at nine thirty that evening. She said goodbye to Olbeck, still hunched over his keyboard, and let herself out of the office, raising a hand to the duty sergeant on the front desk as she left the building.

Settled in the driver's seat, she checked her phone before she drove off. Nothing from Jay. Where the hell was he? She'd now left him three messages. Trying not to worry, she put the key in the ignition, locked her driver side door and drove off.

Kate's new house was situated at the end of a terrace of Victorian buildings at the end of a cul-de-sac. The last streetlight lay twenty feet from her garden gate, meaning her walk up the path to the front door was always slightly nerve-wracking after dark. *I must get an outside light*, she told herself yet again, knowing she'd forget about it once she was through the front door.

As she opened the squeaky little iron gate to the path up to the door, a dark shadow moved. A hand reached for her. There was a moment of cold terror and her hand holding the front door keys came up like a flash; they were a tiny weapon, but it could be the difference between life and death...

She let out her breath in a half-scream as she realised it was her brother.

"Jay, you idiot, you scared the absolute shit out of me!"

Jay said nothing. He stood there, dumbly, shaking his head. Kate could smell the booze on him from three feet away.

"Are you all right?"

He finally spoke. "No, I'm not," he said, in a slurred and teary mumble. "Sis, I'm so not okay. I didn't want to scare you, I didn't know where to go—"

Kate had the front door open now and the hallway light on. She gently pushed Jay into her house before her and turned him to face her. He looked awful: unshaven, red-eyed, hair unbrushed and greasy.

"You've heard about Elodie," she said. It was a statement, not a question.

"Yes," said Jay and burst into tears.

She let him cry, leading him to the sofa and wrapping him up in one of the blankets she kept there. Then she made him a cup of hot chocolate, listening to his sobs gradually tapering off, like a toy winding down. By the time he'd drunk his hot drink, he was dry-eyed again, his chest only occasionally heaving.

"I'm really sorry, Jay," said Kate eventually. "It's awful. You must be feeling desperate."

Jay's mouth crimped. For a moment, she thought he was going to start crying again, but he managed to control himself.

"I can't believe it," he said. He leaned forward and put the mug down on the floor with a shaking hand. "I can't believe it. She was so amazing. Why would anyone do this?"

Kate could only shake her head.

"It shouldn't have happened!" he cried and then buried his face in his hands, sobbing. Kate was reminded of Mr Duncan at the morgue, saying almost those very words.

"Jay," she said gently, after a moment. "We'll need to take a statement from you. I can't do it myself but Mark—you remember Mark?—he can do it for you. You can come to the station with me tomorrow."

Jay shook his head. "I can't. I don't want to have everyone laughing at me for crying, and I can't talk about Elodie without crying." He wiped his face. "I can't, sis."

Kate picked the empty mug from the floor.

"We'll talk about in the morning," she said, before remembering that she had to be at Rawlwood College for the first round of interviews. "Actually, I've got to go out early. You sleep in, have a shower, have some breakfast. We'll talk later when I get back."

When she was finally in bed, she lay wide-eyed in the darkness, staring up at the dim ceiling. She wondered whether Jay was lying awake in the next bedroom too. She hoped not. She rolled on her side, pulling the duvet up to her ear. She hoped she wouldn't dream, but she could sense that the riverbank and the mud and Elodie's white face were lying in wait for her, out there in the dark.

"YOU LOOK AS BAD AS I do," said Olbeck the next morning when he knocked on Kate's door. "Don't tell me you went on a wild bender when you left the office last night."

"I could make a smart remark about that, coming from you," said Kate as she flopped into the passenger seat. "And I won't even start on the 'bender.'"

Olbeck laughed. "So how come you look so rough?"

"I'm not that bad, am I?" Kate flipped down the visor to look in the little mirror and groaned. "Crap. Where's my hairbrush?"

As she brushed her hair, she told Olbeck what had happened last night.

"Poor kid," said Olbeck. "I'll do his statement."

"I told him you would," said Kate. She tied back

her now-neat hair. "I obviously can't do it myself, and he needs someone to be—well—gentle with him."

Olbeck glanced over at her. "Did he say anything about the night she died? Did he see anything?"

Kate dropped her hairbrush back into her bag and snapped it shut.

"He didn't say," she said, shortly. "He wasn't anywhere near her when I left that night, I know that."

"All right, all right," said Olbeck, peering through the windscreen. "You need to talk it through with Anderton later. Where's the bloody turn off for the College?"

The road they were travelling along ran along a high brick wall, ten feet tall. Olbeck spotted the turning, and the car swung into the winding drive of Rawlwood. They drove along through a thin bank of trees before the open lawns of the College began, and the building loomed into view, huge and black in full Gothic splendour.

"My God," said Kate, looking at the turrets and bell tower and the mullioned windows. "It's Hogwarts."

"My school was a bit like this," said Olbeck, slowing down to look.

"Wow. Mine definitely wasn't."

"Yes, well, don't envy me," said Olbeck. Kate was surprised at the bitterness in his voice. "Just because it looks fantastic on the surface doesn't mean it was wonderful underneath."

"True." For a moment, Kate was going to ask Olbeck about his school days. He'd been to private school, she knew that, although she didn't know the specific school he'd attended. He never talked about it.

Kate stared out the window as they approached the visitors' car park. There were little huddles of students here and there, walking back and forth between the buildings, all dressed in the navy and silver uniform: the same uniform worn by Elodie Duncan in the photograph pinned to the crime room whiteboard. Several carried musical instruments in cases. One tiny, redheaded girl was struggling along with a case that was almost bigger than she was. As Kate watched, a grey-haired man, clearly one of the teachers, intercepted her and lifted the case from her small hands. The two of them walked off together, chatting, the case—was it a cello?—between them.

The two of them got out of the car. Kate stood, getting her bearings. It was difficult to know whether there was an unusual amount of activity because of what had happened to Elodie or whether this was just a normal day at Rawlwood. It would be easier to ascertain once they'd spent some time here.

They found the school reception and were

guided to the south wing of the school by a rather superior school secretary, who glided along in front of them, occasionally nodding from side to side and snapping out descriptions such as 'large common room,' 'bursar's room,' and 'dining hall,' as they swept past glimpses of wood-panelled rooms and lofty-ceilinged halls. She delivered them to a much less grand room furnished with a few odd tables and chairs. One of the chairs was occupied by Anderton, who was speed-reading through a pile of papers on the desk in front of him.

"Morning you two," he said without raising his head. Kate and Olbeck stood aside to allow the secretary to sweep back out of the room with an audible sniff.

"Did you get the impression we're not welcome here?" murmured Olbeck.

Kate shrugged.

"We're never welcome anywhere," she said. "Morning, sir."

Anderton pushed the chair back and stood up.

"Right," he said, sweeping the papers away from him. "Now, here's where we'll start—"

There was a commotion outside in the hallway, raised voices, a scrimmage of feet. Two seconds later, a teenage girl came barrelling through the doorway, all long legs and a fall of long brown hair.

"Police—are you the police?" she demanded breathlessly. Without waiting for an answer, she flung her school bag down onto the floor and raised both hands to her head, staring at the officers, wild-eyed. "I've got to talk to you, like, immediately. Are you the police?"

"Yes, we are," said Kate, raising her hands in a 'calm down' gesture. "What's the matter? Do you want to talk to us about—"

"Elodie? Yes, of course I want to talk to you about Elodie! Or rather about *him*. I need to talk to you about *him*!"

The officers looked at one another.

"Who are you talking about?"

The girl looked at them as though they were crazy. Worse, as if they were stupid. "I'm talking about Reuben Farraday," she said. Then she burst into tears. "He always said he'd kill her, and now he has!"

# Chapter Seven

THE THREE OFFICERS STOOD NONPLUSSED for a moment. Then Kate stepped forward, raising her hands in a calming gesture once again. The girl was still sobbing wildly.

"Okay, okay," soothed Kate. "Calm down. What's your name?"

The girl turned out to be Amy Peters, the best friend that Elodie's mother had mentioned. Kate led her to a chair and sat her down, rummaging in her bag for a clean tissue.

The girl only cried for a few more minutes. Then she sat up, threw her hair away from her tear-stained face, and raised both hands to her temples as she took a few deep breaths. There was something stagy about her mannerisms, something not quite natural, as if she was exaggerating genuinely felt emotions. Perhaps she was. Hadn't Mrs Duncan said something about Elodie and Amy having a falling-out?

"Miss Peters?" said Anderton. "Anything you can

tell us will be helpful. You think Reuben Farraday had something to do with Elodie's death?"

Amy stretched her eyes wide.

"Well, of *course*. He was a nightmare to Elodie, simply a nightmare. He used to threaten her *regularly*."

"In what way?"

Amy took a handful of hair and held it back from her head. Kate could tell that she was the kind of girl who used her hair as a form of punctuation: pulling it, twisting it, throwing it back to give emphasis to her words.

"Elodie and Reuben split up about six months ago," she said. "You know that, right? Ever since then—"

"Excuse me, Amy, but why did they split up? What was the reason?"

Amy gave her a look of scorn mixed with incredulity. She had all the superiority of the elite mixed with the ringing self-confidence of the average teenager. Kate was half amused, half annoyed.

"He was possessive," Amy said dramatically. "*Extremely* possessive. Always wanting to know what she was doing and who she was with, never letting her have a moment's peace. For God's sake, she got enough of that at home. Reuben just couldn't accept that she didn't want to spend all her time with him, that she had other friends as well. He was a *nightmare*."

"Other friends? Did Elodie have other boyfriends as well? Is that what you mean?"

Amy stared, her lip curled. "*No*. She wasn't *unfaithful*. Of course not! She just didn't want to spend all her free time with him, God, what little she had. She said she just felt completely suffocated by him, and so she dumped him."

"When was this?"

"I told you. About six months ago. And ever since then, he's been calling and texting and generally being a complete nightmare to her. He wouldn't leave her alone."

"Did her parents know about this?" asked Anderton.

Amy sniffed. "Not really. Elodie always said she could handle it. She didn't believe he was actually serious." For a second, her actressy manner departed, and she was just a young girl with tears in her eyes. Her voice shook a little. "She always said it was just words, that he didn't mean anything by it. I feel awful because I believed her. I thought she knew what she was doing. And now it's too late."

She hung her head, the curtain of hair sweeping forward and hiding her face.

Olbeck cleared his throat. "What sort of threats did he make, Amy?"

There was no response from Amy for a moment.

Kate saw a tear fall from underneath the curtain of hair onto the dusty floor.

"Amy?"

Amy sat up, throwing her hair back and wiping her face.

"I'm sorry," she said. "I'm just very upset. Elodie was my *best friend*."

"What sort of threats did Reuben make, Amy?" asked Olbeck, patiently.

"Terrible ones. When they first split up, he told her he'd kill her."

"You heard him say that?"

"I *saw* it. On Facebook. He deleted it a few hours later, though."

"Did you ever see him physically threaten or assault Elodie?"

Amy pouted. "No, not as such. He used to hang around sometimes and try and talk to her when we got out of class. God, he was such a *stalker*. I don't know why Elodie wasn't more scared of him." Her big blue eyes filled up with tears again. "She should have been. Look what happened."

"Right, Amy, thank you," said Anderton. He put a hand under the girl's arm and helped her up. "DS Olbeck will take a full statement from you now, and you can rest assured we will be questioning Mr Farraday very closely and very soon."

Amy sniffed again and tucked her hair behind her ears. She bent to pick up her school bag.

"I can't believe it," she said, tucking the strap over her shoulder. "First Violet and now this. I sometimes feel this school is *cursed*."

Olbeck led her away to a desk in the corner. Anderton and Kate exchanged glances and Kate cast up her eyes very slightly.

"Teenage girls," she said quietly.

Anderton looked suddenly grim.

"Don't remind me," he said. "I've got two of my own."

"What about Farraday?"

"I think it's about time we pulled him in, don't you?"

"Should I—"

Anderton was already reaching for his jacket. He shook his head. "I need you supervising things here, Kate. I'll handle it. Start working through this list."

"Okay," muttered Kate, dissatisfied. She would rather be out there, taking action, pulling in what sounded like their prime suspect, rather than taking statements from a lot of overly dramatic, snobby students in here. She chastised herself, *Come on, this is important too*. She watched Anderton leave and turned back to see Amy swishing her hair back yet again in the corner. Her teeth clenched with irritation. Then Kate suddenly realised she'd missed something. She walked over to where

Olbeck was taking Amy's statement and waited for an appropriate pause.

"Amy," she said, when she could. "What did you mean by what you said just a moment ago?"

Amy looked at her, wide-eyed. "What do you mean?"

"You said something about the school being cursed. What was that again?"

Amy looked a little ashamed of her dramatic phrase. "Oh, nothing. It was just after what happened to Violet last year—"

"That was it," said Kate. She picked up a chair and joined them at the desk. "What did you mean by that? Who's Violet?"

Amy curled a lock of hair around her fingers, rubbing it against her lips.

"Violet Sammidge," she said, in a small voice. "Don't you remember? She committed suicide last year."

Olbeck and Kate looked at one another.

"I think I remember that," said Olbeck. "In fact, I do remember that. Very sad. She was a pupil here, wasn't she?"

Amy nodded. "We were both in the drama group. She was younger than me, and that's how we met, in drama. She hanged herself in the cloakrooms. It was awful."

"It must have been," said Olbeck. He was looking at Kate in a familiar way. They never asked each other 'is that important?' in front of suspects or witnesses, but she had got to know the look he gave her when he was thinking it. So she got up smartly, thanked Amy and went back to her desk.

It was a long day. Kate interviewed a seemingly endless line of teenage boys and girls and several of Elodie's teachers. Her music teacher, Graham Lightbody, she recognised as the grey-haired man who'd helped the tiny girl carry the huge cello case. He was a soft-spoken, urbane man, given to thoughtful pauses; he took his time to reflect on her questions before answering in measured tones. He too spoke about how special Elodie had been.

"We have a lot of students here with talent, Detective Sergeant. People expect to come to Rawlwood because we nurture the best students. Elodie Duncan was very good. Not the best we've had, I couldn't say that, but I fully expected her to make a great career for herself in the arts."

Kate nodded.

"People with great talent aren't always very happy," she said. "Did Elodie strike you as a happy person? Do you think she was generally content?"

Lightbody smiled. "She was a teenage girl, Detective Sergeant. You're not very old yourself. Surely you can remember being a teenage girl?"

Kate forced a smile. She would be quite happy for most of her teenage years to be wiped from her memory. *No you wouldn't*, whispered a voice. *You wouldn't want to forget him*. As if there was any chance of *that*. She sighed inwardly before turning her attention back to the interview.

"What do you know of Elodie's ex-boyfriend, Reuben Farraday?"

Lightbody raised his eyebrows. "I'm afraid I know nothing of him. He wasn't a pupil here."

"You weren't aware of any threats he'd made against Elodie? Any threatening or violent behaviour?"

"Dear me, no. Not at all. Is he a suspect in her death?"

Kate didn't answer him.

"Did Elodie ever seem scared of anybody?"

"No. Not that I knew. But I'm afraid, Detective Sergeant, that I didn't know her very well. She was a beautiful, talented girl, but as to what she was like as a person, I couldn't say."

Kate nodded. After a few more questions, she brought the interview to a close, thanked Dr Lightbody for his time and handed over her card. Once he'd left the room, she looked over at Olbeck, who was busy writing up the first of many reports.

"That's me done for the day."

Olbeck clicked his pen closed with a flourish.

"Me too. Let's head back and see how Anderton's getting along with young Mr Farraday."

"You read my mind."

# Chapter Eight

BACK AT THE STATION, OLBECK paused outside the interview room. "Coming in?"

Kate shook her head. "I'll just watch."

She went to the viewing room, nodded at Steve, who was monitoring the video feed, and settled down in front of the screen. Reuben Farraday was a good-looking young man with a flopping fringe of dark hair and good cheekbones. Elodie and he must have made a striking couple. Kate looked closely at his face. He was attempting a surly nonchalance, but she could see the fear in his eyes. A solicitor sat next to him—not the duty one but a glossy young woman wearing an expensive trouser suit. His parents were not in attendance; well, now that she considered it, they wouldn't be. He was legally an adult.

"So, Reuben," said Anderton, leaning forward. "I've been told that you and Elodie split up some time ago."

"Yeah," said Reuben.

"Was it an amicable break up?"

Reuben scowled. "It was all right."

Anderton let the silence stretch out for a beat. Then he said, "We've been informed that you made specific and multiple threats to Elodie Duncan once your relationship was over. Can you confirm if that is true?"

Reuben's eyes widened. The solicitor opened her mouth, but he spoke before she could.

"That's not true!"

Anderton looked down at his notes.

"You didn't, for example, threaten to kill her in a post made on Facebook?"

"You don't have to answer that," interposed the solicitor, smoothly.

Reuben was shaking his head. "That's *so* not true. I don't know who told you that. Who told you that?"

Anderton declined to answer him. He sat back and his tone of voice changed. Before he had been brusque; now his voice became gentler, almost fatherly. Kate smiled. She knew the old 'good cop, bad cop' cliché but Anderton was the only officer she knew who managed to flip between the two all by himself.

"Now, Reuben, we've been told that you and Elodie had quite an intense relationship. You were apparently quite serious about one another. It must have come as a shock when your relationship broke down."

Reuben looked at him with a wealth of expression. He might be scared, but underneath it all he was still a teenage boy.

"I don't know who you've been talking to. Elodie and me, we were okay. It wasn't the romance of the century or anything. Half the time—" He paused for a moment. Then he said slowly, "Half the time I just felt sorry for her."

Anderton raised his eyebrows. "What do you mean by that, Reuben?"

Reuben picked at a loose thread on the sleeve of his long black coat. He looked up from under his fringe at Anderton.

"She—Elodie—she had a lot of problems. She was—she could be hard work. But she was cool as well, you know?"

"What kind of problems, Reuben?"

Reuben broke the eye contact. "Oh, I dunno," he said. "She used to cry a lot. I didn't know what was the matter with her half the time."

Anderton nodded as if he understood. "Did she ever confide in you about these problems?"

Reuben shrugged. "Sometimes. Not really. Sometimes she'd start to speak, start to tell me something, and then she'd kind of clam up again. I used to ask her what was wrong when she got upset, and I thought she would be going to tell me but—but something made her stop."

"What do you think was the matter, Reuben?"

"I don't know. I told you, she didn't ever tell me."

Anderton cleared his throat.

"Were you and Elodie sexually involved?"

Reuben flushed, to his obvious mortification. "'Course," he said, uncomfortably. There was a beat of silence.

"But?" said Anderton.

Reuben looked away. Kate could see the heat in his cheeks even over the grainy image of the video feed.

"She didn't—well, she didn't really—" He took a deep breath. "She was kind of mixed up about sex."

"Meaning?"

Reuben dropped his head.

"She was all over the place," he mumbled. "Sometimes she'd be really into it, and sometimes she'd just get angry if I wanted to. I didn't know what was going on half the time."

"Mm-hmm," said Anderton, his face expressionless. Kate wondered if he was thinking about his own teenage girls. "So you're saying she could be a bit—well, a bit of tease?"

"No—not exactly..."

"Did that make you angry, Reuben?"

Reuben shook his head, not vehemently. It

was more convincing than if he had been more emphatic. "I just felt sorry for her," he repeated.

"What do you think?" asked Olbeck when they met in the canteen during a break in the interview.

Kate stirred her coffee.

"I don't know," she said slowly. "On the face of it, there's everything to suggest it was him. Rejected ex-boyfriend, tempestuous relationship. The usual kind of thing. But—"

"I know what you mean," said Olbeck. "I was watching him the whole time. He looked scared but not—not guilty, if you see what I mean."

"A look is not evidence," said Kate, tipping him a wink. "Isn't that what you've said to me before?"

"Ha ha." Olbeck tipped up his mug and drained it. "He's got no alibi, as yet."

"Are you going to charge him?"

"Not sure. Don't think so. I don't think we got enough for it to stick, quite frankly."

"Have you quizzed him about the pregnancy?"

"Not yet. Anderton's keeping that up his sleeve for now. We've swabbed him for DNA obviously."

"Right." Kate picked up her bag and keys and stood up. "I'm off back to the Duncans' house. I need to have a look at Elodie's bedroom."

Kate braced herself before ringing the bell of Rawlwood Cottage. She fully expected Elodie's mother to present the kind of bleached, transparent countenance that only grief could produce. When Genevieve Duncan answered the door, she was certainly pale, her eyes ringed with shadow, but there was something else about her, some other kind of emotion running through her that Kate couldn't quite pinpoint. It shimmered around her like an aura.

"Yes, of course," she replied when Kate asked her if she could see Elodie's room. Mrs Duncan's voice was blank, and her eyes were staring at something in the far distance visible only to her.

"I'll leave everything as I find it," said Kate.

Mrs Duncan nodded. She didn't watch Kate walk up the stairs but instead drifted back into the living room, out of sight.

Elodie's room was large and about as far away from her parents' bedroom as it was possible to be, tucked up into the eaves of the roof. A former attic, the walls sloped sharply downwards from the ceiling, and the only window was small and many-paned. Kate stood in the doorway for a moment, getting the feel of it, snapping on her gloves. It was a pretty room, tastefully decorated. Kate could see that Elodie had stamped her personality over the space in a variety of ways. A huge poster of Jim Morrison covered almost all of one wall. Kate regarded it, feeling as if his dark eyes were watching her. Did teenagers really still listen to the Doors? There was a cork noticeboard next to the poster with a mass of ticket stubs and flyers pinned to it. Kate looked more closely. Glastonbury, Bestival, Isle of Wight festival tickets, some torn-off wrist bands and lots of smaller gig tickets were evident. Well, Elodie had been musical after all, nothing very surprising that she'd enjoyed going to see her favourite bands.

There were photographs on the walls, some framed, some just blu-tacked to the paint. Kate looked at one of Elodie and a girl she recognised as Amy Peters. Both girls looked younger, perhaps thirteen years old: still almost children. They had their arms slung about one another and were laughing, Amy facing the camera, Elodie looking off to the side.

There was a violin lying on the bed, still in its black case. Kate touched it tentatively, then unsnapped the locks and raised the lid. The violin was a beautiful thing, made of polished golden wood. Kate ran a finger softly over its strings. She had never learned to play a musical instrument, and at that moment, she felt the loss keenly. She'd always felt it was something she really ought to do, a skill everyone ought to have to be a fully-rounded person. Then she smiled. Even to herself, she sounded like Miss Bingley in *Pride and Prejudice*. *"A woman must have a thorough knowledge of music, singing, drawing, dancing and the modern languages..."* She thought, *Kate, you've got plenty of other accomplishments, Don't do yourself down.*

There were a few books by the bed, a rather incongruous selection of children's classics. *Winnie the Pooh, Watership Down, The Velveteen Rabbit.* Strange bedtime reading for an eighteen-year-old girl. But perhaps they were just there because they'd always been there since Elodie was a child. Kate picked each book up and shook it upside down to see if anything fluttered out. Nothing. She got on her knees and looked under the bed. You could find surprisingly revealing things under a bed sometimes. Kate remembered the strange photo album that had been under poor Gemma Phillips' bed back in the Charlie Fullman kidnapping case: her first case in Abbeyford. She remembered Charlie's mother, Casey, the little blonde trophy wife. Briefly, Kate wondered what had happened to her. The Fullmans' marriage hadn't lasted much longer than their courtship, if she remembered correctly.

Kate blinked, bringing herself back to the present. There was nothing under Elodie's bed except for an empty shoe box and plenty of dust. Kate got up, dusting off her trousers. She checked Elodie's wardrobe, stood against the only flat, windowless wall at the end of the room. There was something so sad about the clothes of a person who'd recently died; they drooped from their hangers more emptily than normal. Kate moved the hangers apart, checking between each dress and coat and shirt. Shoeboxes were stacked on the floor of the wardrobe. She brought them out into the light, one by one, opening the lid and checking the contents. Nothing untoward. Nothing until she reached the last one, when she pulled off the lid to reveal a plastic bag wrapped tightly round on itself. She could smell the contents nonetheless. She unwrapped it gingerly.

A bag of marijuana, home-grown by the look of it. Kate hefted it in one hand. Several smaller plastic bags of pills. By far the biggest bag in the box was filled with white powder. Kate recalled the manic glitter in Elodie's eyes the night they'd met. The night Elodie had died. Cocaine, then, or some such stimulant. She put all the drugs back in the cardboard box and folded it carefully into a large evidence bag. After a moment's thought, she put the evidence bag into her handbag and zipped it up, hiding it away from Elodie's mother's eyes.

# Chapter Nine

"WELL," SAID OLBECK WHEN SHE showed him her find back at the station. "You can't tell me that's for personal use."

"Not unless she was spending every hour of the day off her face. And I think that would have been obvious to anyone, don't you?"

Olbeck took the bag from her. "We'd better get the usual tests done, just in case."

"I know."

"Find anything else? Anything at all? A diary, or something?"

Kate began to gather the various forms she needed to fill in.

"Teenage girls don't keep diaries any more, do they?" she said. "They just post it all on Facebook."

"True." Olbeck leant back in his chair and pushed his hands through his hair. "The plot thickens. We've got a potential suspect in the ex-boyfriend, and now it seems that our murder victim was a drug dealer."

"We really need to ask her parents about the pregnancy—and this." Kate flourished the bag.

Olbeck nodded. "Let's talk to Anderton. Right now."

As they approached his office, the door stood ajar. Anderton was reclined in his chair behind the large desk, sitting still and staring into space. This was so unusual that Kate stopped dead herself, her hand raised to knock. She stopped short of touching the door as she took in the scene. Anderton was *never* still. Ceaseless, relentless energy was his defining characteristic. For a moment, Kate was infused with a sense of dread. Perhaps Anderton was ill. Really ill. He'd looked so tired lately: tired and somehow diminished.

"What's wrong?" whispered Olbeck behind her.

Kate shook herself mentally.

"Nothing," she said, and knocked.

Anderton took a moment to respond. Then he turned his head disinterestedly.

"Yes?" he asked, after a moment.

"We've had some new developments on the Elodie Duncan case," said Olbeck, sounding a little uncertain. Kate knew he was wondering what was wrong with Anderton just as she was.

There was a moment's silence that hung between the three of them. Then Anderton seemed to take hold of himself.

"Right," he said. He sprang up from his chair and

Kate almost gave a sigh of relief. "Bring me up to speed then. What've you got?"

Kate told him of her find in Elodie's wardrobe.

"Right, right," he said, pacing to the window. He leant both hands on the sill for a moment before turning to face them. "Well done. This could be important."

"We were going to question her parents again. See if they know anything."

"Yes, do that. We're due the tox tests any day now, so we'll be able to see if our girl was partaking as well as supplying."

Kate thought of something.

"Elodie's baby," she said, a little awkwardly. She didn't like discussing things like this with either Olbeck or Anderton—they knew too much of her past. But it could be important..."Is it possible to get a DNA test done on the—the remains of the baby?"

Both men looked at her.

She added. "If we could, we could run the results through the database. See if there's a match on record."

"Mmm," said Anderton. He tousled his hair. "Might be worth a try. Look into it."

"I'll speak to the pathologist," said Kate.

Once they were outside Anderton's room, Kate turned to Olbeck.

"Stop grinning."

"I'm not. I'm smirking."

"I know what you're thinking, and you're wrong."

"Am I?" said Olbeck, innocently. "Sure it's not just an excuse to talk to our young pathologist friend?"

Kate snorted and turned to march off.

"Not everyone's as sex-obsessed as you," was her parting remark, flung over her shoulder.

Olbeck said nothing else on the journey to Rawlwood Cottage but kept the same infuriating grin on his face, humming a little tune. Kate tried to ignore him. Then she asked him whether he knew if there was anything wrong with Anderton.

The grin dropped from his face immediately.

"Why do you ask?"

"You know," said Kate. "He's not himself. There's something bugging him—or he's not well."

"I don't know," said Olbeck, worriedly. "He hasn't said anything to me."

"Hmm." Kate drew up outside the Duncan's house. "Okay, we're here. Do you want to take the lead, or shall I?"


"Drugs?"

Mr Duncan looked as if someone had just punched him in the face. He had been standing, but at the word, he sat down suddenly on the sofa behind him, as if his legs had suddenly given way.

"I'm sorry, Mr Duncan," said Olbeck. "I assume

you weren't aware that your daughter had a large quantity of drugs in her bedroom? That she could well have been supplying them to others?"

Mr Duncan was shaking his head from side to side slowly, seemingly dazed.

"I had—I had no idea," he said. "I can't—can't believe it. Surely there must have been some mistake? Elodie...Elodie wasn't like that."

Kate was looking keenly at Genevieve Duncan.

"Mrs Duncan?" she prompted. The woman sat with eyes cast down, picking at the worn threads of the armchair once again. How many hours had she sat there, pulling threads from the arm in ceaseless anxiety?

"Mrs Duncan," said Kate again, more firmly. "Is this news to you?"

For a moment, she thought the woman would refuse to answer. Mrs Duncan put her hand up to her face, covering her eyes in a characteristic gesture.

"Mrs Duncan?"

"I found something," Mrs Duncan burst out. She lowered her shaking hand. "Just once. A plastic packet with something in it. I don't know what it was. Some sort of white powder. I'm not stupid...I—" She pinched her trembling lips together for a moment with her fingers, and then released them. "I asked Elodie about it."

"You asked her?"

"Yes. I had to, didn't I? My own daughter..." Mrs

Duncan slumped against the back of the chair, her hands falling limply to her lap.

After a moment, Kate asked, "What happened?"

Mrs Duncan stared into space.

"Mrs Duncan?"

"She got angry," said Mrs Duncan, dully. "The way she always did. She had so much...*rage* inside her. I don't know where it came from... She got angry, and then she laughed and said that I didn't know anything. That I didn't understand and never had."

"Did you ever find anything else?"

"No. I never did. But I didn't look. Who knows what else she had in her room, what she could have been hiding?"

Kate knew the time was right for the second question, but she quailed a little at asking it. You needed the hide of rhinoceros to do this job, sometimes. Was that what was wrong with Anderton? Could he just not face the emotional payback any more?

Olbeck pre-empted her. He did that sometimes, knowing almost telepathically when to take over and face the outcome, letting Kate gather her defences together once more.

"I'm sorry to cause you both any more distress, but I have another question for you. Where you aware that Elodie was ten weeks pregnant when she died?"

Mrs Duncan made a noise, a kind of half-grunt, half-shout. She flinched back as if Olbeck had shouted at her.

"Oh my God," was all she said and then the tears began again. Mr Duncan gathered her into his arms, rocking and crooning to her like a child.

Olbeck gave them a couple of minutes. Then he asked the question again.

"No, of course I didn't know," Mrs Duncan almost shouted. Mr Duncan sat beside her, shaking his head.

"Mr Duncan? Did Elodie confide in you?"

He flinched. "No. No, she didn't. I had no idea, no idea about any of this." There was some kind of undercurrent to his voice, and it took Kate a few moments to realise what it was—anger. "I had no idea what she was up to. She didn't tell me anything." He glanced at his wife. "She didn't tell *us* anything."

"Who was it?" Mrs Duncan sat up, holding her arms across her body like a woman expecting a physical blow. Her voice was shaking so much it was hard for Kate to understand what she was saying.

"What do you mean, Mrs Duncan?" asked Kate.

"Who was the father?"

"We don't yet know, I'm afraid."

"Yet?" said Mr Duncan, his face grey. "You mean you *will* know?"

"No, we can't promise that, sir, I'm sorry. There's a possibility that we'll be able to run various tests that might give us a DNA profile, but it's not certain. I wouldn't want to give you false hope. Even if we do get a DNA sample, there's no way to know anything more unless we have an equivalent record on file."

"I see," said Mr Duncan. He put one shaking hand up to his forehead. "I don't know how much more of this we can take."

"We're very sorry," said Olbeck. "We'll keep you informed every step of the way."

# Chapter Ten

"Can you drop me back at my place?" Kate asked as they were on their way home. "In fact, why don't you come in? We'll pick up Jay and take him back to the station to do his statement."

Olbeck concurred. As they drew up outside Kate's house, she realised someone else had parked in her driveway.

"That's not your car, is it?" asked Olbeck.

"No, it's not." Kate got out of the car, puzzled. The car was a large estate car, old but well-kept. She didn't recognise it. Halfway to the front door, it opened and out came someone she wasn't expecting or prepared to see: her mother.

"Kelly!"

Her mum flung her arms around Kate. Taken by surprise, Kate could only manage a feeble "Hi, Mum. What are you doing here?" in response.

Her mother didn't seem to notice her lukewarm greeting. She released Kate and stood back, beaming. Kate almost goggled. Her mother looked...

well, *groomed* was the only word for it: her hair done, make-up on her face, her clothes different to the usual stained and worn tracksuit that Kate was used to seeing her wear. She looked *smart*, a word hitherto never associated with Mary Redman.

Kate pulled herself together.

"What are you doing here, Mum?" she asked. "Did Jay let you in?"

"Thought we'd see your new place, didn't we? I said to Peter, 'We may as well go and see Kelly while we're here,' and so we all came over. Very nice too, Kelly, shame you didn't invite us over before."

A man appeared in the doorway behind Mary. He was portly, middle-aged, with a neatly-trimmed beard. He was wearing brown cord trousers and a fisherman's jumper.

"Here he is," exclaimed Mary. "Here she is, Peter. This is Kelly."

Kate forced a smile. She shook hands with Peter, debating whether to insist that he call her Kate. She realised Olbeck was standing behind her, and she introduced him to her mother and Peter. Thank God she'd already told Olbeck she'd changed her name in her teens. As it was, he was not above calling her Kelly when he wanted to annoy her.

"Pleased to meet you," said Peter. He had a kind of tweedy, avuncular air about him, which was quite appealing. What *was* he doing with her mother? Kate found herself shepherding them all back into the house where she had a second surprise: her two younger half-sisters Courtney and Jade were in the garden with Jay, smoking cigarettes.

"It's the full family contingent," she said to Olbeck, trying to make a joke of it. He hadn't met any of her siblings before except Jay.

"Alright, sis," said Courtney, coming over and giving her a smoky hug. "When are you gonna get some real furniture?"

"What do you mean?" asked Kate, realising with a jolt that her seventeen-year-old sister was now taller than her. And Jade—she hadn't seen Jade for nearly a year. Her youngest sister was now a large, plump young woman, and she was wearing a pair of straining leggings and a top that did nothing to hide a mountainous pair of breasts. Try as she might, Kate could not suppress the thought that her fourteen-year-old sibling looked cheap and tarty. She gave Jade an extra warm hug to try and atone for her thoughts.

"Well, it's a bit old, innit?" Courtney looked disdainfully at the worn leather sofa that Kate found so comfortable.

"Oh well," said Kate rather helplessly. "I will when I get around to it."

She made tea for those who wanted it: Peter, Olbeck, and herself. Jay had stood silently through the greetings and tumult of the female Redmans, and he was now sat at the kitchen table with his eyes cast down. Kate wished she could get rid of everyone so she could talk to him.

Olbeck saved her. While Kate was showing her mother and Peter, at their insistence, round the house and into the garden, she saw Olbeck talking quietly to Jay. After about ten minutes, he came over to tell her he was taking her brother to the station to make his statement.

"Statement?" screeched Mary. "What's he done?"

"Nothing, Mum, I'll explain later," said Kate hurriedly, seeing Jay flinch. She squeezed his arm as he went past, hoping to catch his eye, but he flashed her a quick half smile and then he and Olbeck were gone.

Jade, Courtney and Mary surrounded her, bombarding her with questions.

"It's nothing," said Kate desperately. "He's just a witness, that's all. It's nothing—"

"Now, now," said Peter, unexpectedly. "Don't badger the poor girl. Why don't we all sit down and listen to what Kate has to tell us, if she's willing and able to?"

Mary shut up instantly. Courtney and Jade subsided after Peter raised his hand in a 'shushing' gesture and motioned for Kate to speak.

While Kate was explaining what had happened— all that she could say about the case—a small part of her was mulling over Peter's presence. Her mother was clearly smitten with him, and the girls seemed to like him. He seemed a nice enough man. But what was the attraction for *him*? Did he really like her mother? If so, *why*? Kate hated herself for thinking like that, but she'd faced the facts about her mother a long time ago. Mary Redman had a drinking problem, and she was feckless, short-tempered and unreliable. Where was the attraction in that?

They all left soon after. Kate shook hands with Peter at the door of her house as they were making their goodbyes.

"I didn't ask you how you came to be in the vicinity," she said. "Do you live around here?"

"Yes, duck—not far from here. Burton Abbot. You must come and visit me sometime."

"That would be lovely," said Kate politely. "I'm pretty busy with work at the moment, though. What do you do?"

"Me? I'm a driving instructor." Peter laughed. "Bit nerve-wracking at times, but I do enjoy it."

Courtney and Jade were getting into the back of Peter's car. Kate gestured to it.

"Do you use that for lessons? It looks quite unscathed."

Peter put an arm around Mary and began to shepherd her towards the passenger seat.

"No, I've got something a bit more modern for the learners," he said. "You might even have seen it around. Bright yellow Mini. Easy for other drivers to spot—and avoid! Pete Buckley's yellow peril, they call it."

Kate smiled and waved as they drove away. Once they were gone, she went quickly back inside to her desk and scribbled 'Peter Buckley, Burton Abbot' on a piece of paper and put it in her bag.

She stood for a moment in the hallway, hesitating. Then she climbed the stairs and went straight to the cupboard where she'd put Jay's picture. She drew it out carefully. It no longer induced in her a sense of nausea and panic, despite the resemblance to the crime scene photographs she'd seen every day at the office. She looked harder at the picture, noting that the leaves of the trees in the background were a bright, fresh green. There were wildflowers growing on the banks of the river. Kate noticed something she'd never noticed before: the crown of tiny daisies wound about Elodie's tangled blonde hair. Of course, she was supposed to be Ophelia, wasn't she?

*"There is a willow grows aslant a brook*

*That shows his hoar leaves in the glassy stream*

*There with fantastic garlands did she come*

*Of crow-flowers, nettles, daisies, and long purples..."*

Kate propped the picture against the wall and sat back on her haunches. It was coincidence, that was all. There was nothing to be afraid of. She would tell Anderton tomorrow, she told herself, and she ignored the tiny quake of fear that followed.

# Chapter Eleven

"COCAINE," SAID ANDERTON. "AND MARIJUANA, but we don't care so much about that. The tox tests are back. Our girl tested positive for cocaine, which given DS Redman's discovery the other day, probably doesn't come as a great surprise to most of you."

He stopped, swivelled on one foot and began to retrace his steps. His team watched him, ranged around the room in their various seats. He tapped Elodie's school picture as he walked by it.

"Now, you're not telling me that an eighteen-year-old private school girl, daughter of the headmaster no less, is the sole mastermind behind the supply of Class A drugs to her school mates. Because I just don't believe it."

"Me neither," said Olbeck. "Who gave it to her?"

"Exactly, Mark. There's someone behind all this."

Kate was shuffling the various copies of the witness statements already taken from Elodie's schoolmates.

"Several people mention an older boyfriend. Well, they mention a man they'd seen with Elodie a couple of times." She hesitated. "I think I saw him myself, if it's the same guy. He was older than her, definitely older."

Anderton looked at her.

"Yes, you've mentioned him. What else can you tell us?"

Kate shrugged. "Unfortunately, sir, not much. I only saw him for a moment or so."

"Did you recognise him?"

Kate lifted her shoulders up again. "It's funny but when I first saw him, I *did* think I recognised him. Then I realised he just seemed familiar. I thought I might have arrested him at one time and that's where I knew him from. That's all. No name, nothing like that."

Anderton swung on his heel again.

"Well, we must find him. I have the feeling this mystery man is the key to what happened to Elodie. Find him, and we're a giant step forward." He pointed a finger at Theo. "Theo, go through the statements that mention him. Talk to those witnesses again, get them to see if they can remember any more. Kate, go with him. See if what they tell you tallies with what you remember of this man."

Kate nodded. She looked across at Theo, and he winked at her, which made her grin.

"Jane, where are we with the CCTV?" asked Anderton.

Jane hopped off the desk and handed over a mass of papers. "Several interesting sightings," she said, pointing to something on the camera printouts. "Two men here, and again here. Unfortunately we can't see their faces."

"Bloody hoodies," grumbled Anderton. "Do we have any sightings of Elodie?"

"Yes, she was on the camera outside the pub, leaving with a man—probably the one you saw her with, Kate—and walking into the car park. Unfortunately the camera on that area of the car park was on the blink and we've got nothing definite. She could have got into a car, she could have driven off somewhere, or she could have walked away. There are no cameras on that section of the river footpath."

"Shame. Okay, this'll do for now. What else?" He scanned the board and his scribbled notes. "Kate! DNA tests?"

"Sorry, sir, I haven't had a chance. I'll ring the pathologist today." She could see Olbeck grinning at her from across the room and mouthed 'sod off' at him.

"You won't have a chance *today*, you'll be out with Theo. Jerry, you do it. Right, what else? What else?" He came to a standstill in front of the boards, both hands churning his hair. "Mark, Rav, you're with me. We need to get young Reuben back in for more questioning. He's not off my hit-list yet, not by a long shot. And at some point. we need to go back and question our jogger—what's his name? Deedham."

Rav stuck his hand up smartly.

"We've done that, sir. Jerry and I went to see him yesterday. Still insists he didn't know Elodie Duncan. He's regularly seen jogging on that stretch of the riverbank, and his wife also insists he didn't know our victim. We did a bit of digging, but there's nothing. Nothing at all."

"Great," said Anderton. "I suppose his wife alibied him too?"

Rav nodded. Anderton threw up his hands in exasperation.

"Fine, we'll wash him out for now. What about Reuben Farraday? He got an alibi yet?"

"His parents," said Jane. She shrugged. "For what that's worth."

"Fine, fine," said Anderton through gritted teeth. "So we're absolutely no further forward than we were. Bring him in, anyway and let's get on with it. Oh—" Anderton sagged suddenly, as if struck by an unpleasant thought. His hands dropped to his side. His team stared at him.

After a moment, he went on.

"I can't actually, I've got a meeting. Damn. You

two carry on and report back. I can't get out of this one. Unfortunately."

There was a moment's silence. Kate wondered if anyone else had caught the bleak look that flashed across Anderton's face, just for a split second. Then it was gone, and he was calling out his goodbyes, *carry on team, good work* and striding out the door.

Olbeck was looking after Anderton with a worried look on his face.

"Hey, Mark," said Kate, as much to distract him as because she wanted to know. "I hope you didn't find my family too overwhelming."

Olbeck turned to her, smiling. "Course not. Your brother's a nice kid."

"How was his statement?" asked Kate, speaking casually despite the sudden jump of anxiety that she felt.

"Quite straightforward." Olbeck sat down and rummaged through the paperwork on his desk. "Here you go. You can read it at your leisure."

"Thanks." Kate took it and skimmed it quickly, inwardly quaking. But there was nothing there that jumped out. Nothing that could be construed as... dangerous. She blew out her cheeks and put the paper in her desk drawer to read properly when she had some more time. There was something else that she had to do—what was it now? Oh yes...before she pulled the scrap of paper from her bag, she asked Olbeck another question.

"What did you think of Peter?"

Olbeck was texting again. "Who?"

"My mum's new man. The bloke with the beard."

Olbeck looked up from his phone. "I didn't really notice him much, to be honest. He seemed okay."

"Hmm."

Olbeck's eyes narrowed. "Why?"

"Oh, nothing." Kate swung her chair back and forth a little. "It's just—why would someone like that..."

"Yes?"

Kate cringed inwardly as she said it. "Why would a man like that be interested in my mum? What's he after?"

Olbeck stared at her for a long moment. Then he put down his phone.

"I don't understand you," he said. "I know this is a weird thing to say to a detective, but you are *so* suspicious. What do you mean, what's he after? Why can't he just be after your mum?"

"You don't understand," muttered Kate. She swung her chair away from him, avoiding his accusing gaze. "You don't know my mum. Why would someone like him be interested in someone like her?"

Olbeck scoffed. "Listen to you. I've only met your mum once, and she's not that bad, from what I could see. She's quite attractive. I can see why he'd be attracted to her."

"*Quite attractive?*"

"Yes." He grinned suddenly. "You look quite like her, actually."

"I do not!"

Kate fought a childish urge to put her fingers in her ears. She was suddenly furious with Olbeck. How dare he say that, how dare he compare her to her mother? *I am nothing like her*. She turned her back on him, picked the piece of paper out of her bag and fired up the various databases that she needed.

"What are you doing?"

She ignored Olbeck's question. She looked down at the piece of paper in her hand. Peter Buckley, Burton Abbot. Then, ignoring the voice inside that told her she was being unreasonable, suspicious, *paranoid*, she typed Peter's name into the appropriate fields.

"Are you checking up on him?"

"Shut up, Mark."

"You are, aren't you? Jesus Christ."

"Shut up, Mark."

Over the other side of the room, she could see Theo beckoning. She gave him a 'five minutes' gesture and turned her attention back to the screen. Nothing. No match. No records. A great swamping wave of shame washed over her. What on Earth did she think she was doing?

"You see?" said Olbeck from behind her shoulder.

"Oh, shut up."

She got up and grabbed her bag and coat. Theo was waiting for her by the office door.

"Nutter," said Olbeck, in a not unkind tone, as she walked off.

Theo drove. Kate hadn't worked alone with him for some time, and it felt rather odd to be sat next to someone who wasn't Olbeck. There had been a time, not long after she joined the team in Abbeyford, when Theo had taken her for a drink after work and made a pretty direct pass at her. She'd turned him down (not without some regret— he really *was* very good looking) and there had been a dreadfully strained couple of months before Theo had got himself a new girlfriend and had apparently forgiven her. All that was water under the bridge now. Kate liked him very much; he had the cockiness of attractive youth but was also whip-smart, ambitious and good at his job.

They presented themselves at the headmaster's office on arrival. Kate wasn't sure he would be there; perhaps he was still too grief-stricken to come to work. But after a moment's wait in the superior secretary's office, Mr Duncan came outside to shake their hands and greet them in a subdued fashion. He looked as if he'd aged twenty years in the few days since Kate had last seen him.

"Of course you may use the room," he said, in answer to their question. "You must have free rein..."

He trailed off, staring past Kate's shoulder and out of the window. Then he seemed to recollect himself.

"I'm sorry. Please go ahead with whatever you have to do."

"Poor bastard," whispered Theo as they left the room. Kate nodded.

She thought she knew the way to the room they'd used before, but she was mistaken. After several wrong turns down wood-panelled corridors, she stopped, irritated.

"This place is a bloody *maze*."

Theo gestured.

"I recognised that bit back there."

They retraced their steps to a small foyer, where glass fronted cases displayed various trophies and awards. There were several large class photographs, children lined up in rows with the teachers standing behind them. The names of the children were printed underneath. As Kate hesitated, wondering where to go, a name caught her eye.

"Violet Sammidge. Look, Theo. That's the girl who committed suicide here last year."

They both looked. Violet Sammidge had been a gawky, large-eyed girl with a mass of frizzy brown hair. She stared out of the photograph, grinning anxiously. Kate felt a flicker of something too intangible to name. A fluttering of clarity in the far corners of her comprehension, something so brief that it was gone almost before she could acknowledge it.

"Ah, Detective Sergeant," said an urbane voice by her shoulder. She turned to find Graham Lightbody, the grey-haired teacher, standing by her with an armful of files.

He saw what they had been looking at.

"What a tragedy that was," he said. His face contracted briefly. "I don't believe we've got over it yet."

"You taught Violet?"

"Taught her? My dear, she was my protégé. A quite exceptional talent. I was just devastated—" He broke off abruptly, staring at the photograph of the dead girl. After a moment, he went on. "She was an unhappy child, I could see that. Her parents had not long gone through a very messy and painful divorce when she began her lessons with me. I don't know how much I helped..." He trailed off again. "Not enough, it seems. Not nearly enough."

There was a moment's silence. Then Mr Lightbody pulled the files closer to his chest.

"You'll have to excuse me, Detective Sergeant. I have a class now."

He nodded to Theo and set off down the corridor, his footsteps echoing back from the panelled walls.

# Chapter Twelve

THEY EVENTUALLY FOUND THE ROOM they were
looking for and settled down to go through the
statements.

"Who's first?" asked Theo

Kate read the name on the first statement and
groaned.

"Amy Peters." She gave Theo a wry look. "You'll
enjoy this one."

"Why?"

"She's young, lively and beautiful."

Theo brightened up. "Let's get started then."

Amy Peters entered the room in a slightly less
dramatic fashion than she had the time before.
There was still a hint of staginess about her, and
the hair-tossing had not noticeably decreased.

"Of *course* I saw Elodie with a man. Several
times. I told you this before."

"Perhaps you could just take us through it again,
Amy," said Kate pleasantly. She kept her eyes on the
girl's face. What had her relationship with Elodie

*really* been like? Best of friends or something else? It was hard to see through the theatrical gloss of Amy's behaviour.

Amy cast Theo a flirtatious glance from underneath lowered lashes, smiled, and then turned back to Kate.

"I saw him a couple of times with Elodie. He was tall and pretty fit if you like the older man thing." She giggled and threw back her hair. "I even asked Elodie about him once, but she wouldn't tell me anything."

"Do you know when she met him? How long she had known him?"

Amy shook her head. "I told you, I only saw her with him a handful of times. Once, outside the school gates, she got into his car. And once in town. They were going into a pub."

"Which one?"

"I don't know. I can't remember. Just some dive, nowhere nice."

"Where was this pub?"

"On Castle Street, I think. I'd never actually been there myself." She cast up her eyes to the ceiling. "Elodie always did like slumming it."

The words, spoken in her beautiful RP accent, sounded even more disdainful than Amy had probably meant them to. Kate could see Theo's brows drawing down and knew that Amy had lost her admirer. *Arrogant little bitch.* Even as Kate was thinking it, she was chastising herself inwardly for using the words.

Kate let the silence draw out just a moment too long for comfort. It was a technique she'd seen Anderton use to effect more than once. Then she asked another question.

"Can you tell us something about Elodie herself, Amy? She's still a mystery to us. Her parents don't seem to have the first clue about what she was up to."

Amy looked at her, wide-eyed and innocently.

"What do you mean?"

"Did you ever see Elodie take drugs?"

The beautiful, wide eyes blinked.

"Drugs? Elodie?" Amy's gaze dropped away. "No. No, I didn't."

"Did Elodie ever sell *you* any drugs?" asked Kate, bluntly.

"No," said Amy. She gave her hair an indignant toss.

"Really?" said Kate. "You won't get into trouble for telling me the truth."

Amy looked at her directly.

"Elodie never sold me any drugs. I swear on my mother's life."

Kate held her gaze.

"Never, Amy?"

"I told you, no. Drugs are for losers." Amy tossed

her head again. "We don't have that sort of thing around here."

"Balls, they don't," said Theo after the interviews, when they were walking back to the car and discussing what they'd heard.

"I agree with you," said Kate. "I'm pretty sure Amy's lying. She's got the faux-naivety thing down quite nicely though. I'll give her credit for being quite a good actress."

"We're still no nearer finding out who this older guy is."

Kate shrugged. "We know that Amy did actually *see* him. We can ask around at the pub she talked about. If we manage to get a name, we might be able to pull up a photograph."

Back at the station, Kate was caught up in the reams of paperwork that she'd been neglecting. She barely had time to grab a canteen sandwich and a hurried cup of tea, let alone have time to do any more thinking. After three hours of solid desk work, she stretched, yawned and sat back in her chair, grimacing at the ache in her shoulders. Opening her desk drawer to grab a fresh pen, she caught sight of the paper that Olbeck had given her that morning: Jay's statement. She took it up and read through it carefully, noting particularly what Jay had said he had been doing between the crucial hours during which the murder had taken place. Nothing very illuminating. He'd apparently been with one of the band members—the singer, Tom Hough—and they seemed to have spent a couple of hours wandering around Arbuthon Green, smoking cigarettes and 'losing track of time.' There was no mention of Elodie after she'd left the pub with her older companion. Kate frowned, thinking hard, tapping the paper on her desk. Then she made up her mind.

Anderton's office door was shut. This was so unusual that Kate stopped, momentarily wrong-footed. Of course, he shut the door when he had a meeting with one or more of the upper echelons of the police hierarchy. Kate bent awkwardly down to see if she could see more than one pair of feet beyond the opaque section of glass that ran along his office wall. Nothing. Was he even in? It was late—perhaps he'd left already. She knocked, hesitantly at first, and then louder when there was no response.

"Come in," was the quiet response to her second knock. Kate popped her head around the door. Anderton was sitting at his desk and for the strangest moment, Kate had the impression that he'd just raised his head from his hands.

"Yes, Kate?"

"I've got some more information for you

regarding the case, sir," she said a little nervously. She hadn't really planned out what she was going to say. For a moment, she wished she'd gone away without knocking and left her revelation for another day. Anderton was looking at her with an expression she couldn't read.

"You've found Elodie's boyfriend?"

"Not yet, sir, no. We're further forward there, a bit. I wanted to tell you about something..." Kate hesitated, feeling something like a tremor of unease, a premonition of how this conversation would go. Then she plunged on.

Anderton said nothing as she told him of the picture her brother had painted, how the crime scene had reminded her of the picture but that it had to be coincidence, particularly as the body had actually been found in the river. How Jay and Elodie were friends but nothing more than that. How she had wondered whether it was even worth mentioning but thought she should for completeness. Anderton still said nothing. By now, Kate was gabbling, filling up the silence and feeling the metaphorical temperature in the room drop from neutral to icy to twenty below freezing.

Eventually she managed to stop herself speaking. There was a long moment of silence before Anderton opened his mouth.

When he did finally speak, his voice was ominously quiet.

"Why have you taken days to tell me this, DS Redman?"

At the use of her full formal title, Kate realised that Anderton was furious. She tried to speak calmly, hiding the fact that her heart was beating fast.

"I didn't think it was particularly important sir. I'm sorry—"

Anderton still spoke in that ominously quiet voice.

"Your brother painted a picture that closely resembles the crime scene of our murder victim—your brother, who was one of the last people known to have seen Elodie Duncan alive. Your brother, who by all accounts is infatuated with the victim. You knew all this days ago—and you didn't think it was particularly important?"

Kate swallowed. She knew she was, conversationally at least, one step away from plunging over a precipice.

"I...when I found that the body had been pulled from the river—it had to have been a coincidence—"

The ground crumbled beneath her. Anderton catapulted himself up from his chair, leaning over his desk to shout into her face.

"Coincidence, my arse! You kept this from me deliberately, Redman. You were protecting your brother—"

"I wasn't," gasped Kate, fighting the urge to run from the room.

"Don't lie to me—"

"I told him to make a statement! I, I encouraged him to come forward—"

"Why didn't you tell me about this earlier?"

"I—I didn't—"

"*Why*?"

Kate shut her eyes for a moment, unable to help it. She shook her head, unable to answer.

Anderton sat back down, breathing heavily. After a moment, he spoke quietly, but with an added, hissing emphasis.

"I don't care if it was your brother who did this. I wouldn't care if it was your *son*."

Kate flinched as if he'd slapped her. What was worse, after the initial shock of the words he'd used, was the realisation that he'd said them deliberately to hurt her; he had used the words he knew would cause her maximum pain.

Silence fell. After a moment, Anderton reached for the telephone on his desk. Kate kept her eyes on the floor, unable to look him in the face.

"Jerry," said Anderton in the receiver. "I'm swearing a warrant for the arrest of Jason Redman. I want him picked up and brought back here to answer some questions about Elodie Duncan's murder."

"No!" said Kate, unable to help herself. "It wasn't him! He wouldn't do it—"

Anderton ignored her.

"Quick as you can, Jerry, thank you. That's all for now." He put the receiver down.

Kate dug her fingers into her leg, willing herself not to cry. When she could trust her voice, she asked, "Can I sit in on the interview, sir?"

"Are you actually insane? Do you not see how inappropriate that would be?"

Kate did see it, of course she did. She nodded, eyes down. "What about Mark?"

"Don't make me laugh. You probably roped him into not saying anything too."

Kate gasped, stung into indignation by the unfairness of that remark. "He knew nothing about it, nothing."

"So *you* say. God help us, it's come to this that I can't trust my own officers."

Kate stood up, trembling. She'd made a mistake, but she was human. Jay was her *brother*. She'd never known Anderton like this. He could be brusque and demanding—but he'd never before been cruel. He'd never before been unfair.

"I am truly sorry, sir," she said. "I made a mistake and for that I apologise. But I was not trying to shield my brother, and I am not someone that you can't trust. And neither is Mark. And you know that. You *know* that, sir."

Anderton looked at her, expressionless.

"What's wrong with you?" Kate asked, and there

was real puzzlement and concern in her voice, something that caused Anderton's granite face to flicker.

He leant forward and put his face in his hands.

"Get out," he said, his voice muffled by his fingers.

# Chapter Thirteen

KATE WALKED BACK TO HER desk. Oddly, she no longer felt like crying. It was as if she'd been blasted numb, as if she had walked away from a serious accident apparently unscathed. But deep within her, something had been badly damaged. She sat down at her desk carefully.

She couldn't think about Jay yet. Whenever he came into her mind, it was his younger face that she remembered, the face of the little boy she'd loved and cared for over so many years. The thought of him being arrested twisted something deep inside her. Would he run or try to run? Would they handcuff him or would he come quietly? *Was he guilty?* She mimicked Anderton, putting her face in her hands to try and block out the thought.

Someone put a warm hand on her shoulder and she jumped.

"What's up?" said Olbeck, quietly.

Kate shook her head. Over Olbeck's shoulder,

she could see the clock on the wall, its hands pointing to eight o'clock.

"Are you knocking off soon?" she asked.

Olbeck was regarding her with a worried look on his face. "I was," he said absently. "Why, are you heading home?"

Kate nodded. She thought of her silent house, Jay's things in the spare bedroom, perhaps a sign of a struggle.

"Why don't you come home with me?" she said. "Come and have dinner at my place."

"Well," said Olbeck, "I did sort of have something planned—"

"Please." *Don't leave me on my own.*

Olbeck looked at her appraisingly. Then he nodded. "Okay. Why not?"

As soon as he'd agreed, Kate felt guilty, guilty and ashamed of her own weakness.

"Oh, it's okay...if you've got something planned—"

Olbeck patted her shoulder again. "S'alright," he said. "I don't like him much anyway, to be honest. Might do me good to have a quiet night in."

"Thanks," said Kate, gratefully.

"Tell me all about it on the way home."

"Thanks," said Kate again, and she meant it from the bottom of her heart.

They bought takeaway Chinese on the way home and stopped off at the corner shop for a bottle of wine (for Olbeck) and a bottle of elderflower cordial (for Kate). There was a small section of DVDs for hire in one aisle of the shop and Olbeck stopped in front of the display.

"Let's get a film."

Kate cast a disinterested eye over the plastic cases. Then she realised that watching something mindless might actually take her mind of the terrible images that kept circulating.

"What do you want to watch?" she asked, praying he wouldn't choose something crime-related or anything gory.

Mark ran a finger along the cases and picked one out.

"How about this? British rom-com. Something fluffy."

"Fine," said Kate. She saw once again Anderton's face as he buried it in his hands. She blinked and that image was replaced by one of Jay in a police cell, young and small and scared. *Stop thinking about it.* She realised she was staring into space. Olbeck was already at the counter, paying for the DVD.

Once they were back at her house, she turned on the oven and put the takeaway containers inside it to keep warm. Then she told Olbeck to follow her and led him up to the hallway cupboard on the landing upstairs, where she'd stored the painting.

"Here," she said. "What do you think? I mean, really think?"

Olbeck took it from her silently and regarded it

intently. She watched his face, not knowing quite what it was she wanted to see there.

"It's not—not that bad, is it?" she said after the silence stretched too long.

"I don't know," said Olbeck in a low voice. "I don't know. In one way, it takes your breath away, how close it is but yet—when I look at it more closely, I can see that, well, there's nothing really much there."

"Yes, I think so too," said Kate. "The more you look at it the more you realise it's *not* much alike at all. Don't you?"

"Mmm." Olbeck sounded less convinced that she would have liked. After a moment, he propped the picture back against the wall and stood up.

"Come on, I'm starving. Let's eat and watch the film."

Back in the living room, Olbeck began to fiddle about with the DVD player.

"Can I make a fire?" he asked eagerly, like a small boy. Kate was amused, in spite of herself.

"Of course. Knock yourself out. I'll get the food."

Olbeck got the DVD working and knelt to build the fire. Once it was crackling to his satisfaction, he sat back on Kate's sofa and put his feet up. He looked around the neat, cosy, nicely-decorated room. It was funny—when he'd been with Joe, he couldn't stand to be in this kind of warm domestic setting; it made him want to run screaming down to the nearest dodgy bar and never go home again. At Kate's, it somehow felt different. Perhaps it was because he was just a visitor. *She'll make someone a wonderful wife someday*, he thought and decided with a grin to tell her that when she came back into the room, mainly to see the outraged look on her face.

Kate came back with a plate full of food and a glass of wine for him, but by that time, the moment had passed. She brought in her own tray and they began to watch the film.

"This is shite," said Olbeck, after about twenty minutes had passed.

"It's certainly low-budget," said Kate. She pushed listlessly at the remaining food on her plate—she'd hardly touched anything.

"It's pretty dated, isn't it? Look at the mobiles they're carrying."

Kate scoffed. "Trust you to notice that."

"I'm just going to the little boy's room. Don't bother stopping it."

Kate pushed a forkful of cold rice into her mouth and chewed slowly, staring at the screen, not so much because she was interested in what was happening, more that she couldn't be bothered to look away. The film changed scenes. Her eyes widened. Suddenly she sat bolt upright and choked.

Olbeck was halfway up the stairs when he heard Kate yell. He arrived back in the living room five seconds later, wide-eyed.

"What the hell? What's the matter?"

Kate was spluttering, covered in half-chewed rice. She clawed frantically for the remote, stabbing her finger at the screen.

"It's him, it's him! The guy, the man—it's him!"

"What the hell?"

"There, *there*. It's him, it's our guy. The one with Elodie. Look there—"

She paused the DVD. The actor on screen froze, staring out from the screen.

Kate wiped the last remaining grains of rice away from her mouth.

"Are you sure?" asked Olbeck.

"I'm sure. It's him. My God."

They looked at one another in shock. "I can't believe it. He's an actor. No wonder he looked familiar."

"He *was* an actor," said Olbeck, checking the back of the DVD cover. "I was right. This film's twelve years old. He might not still be an actor."

Kate was staring at the screen.

"It's definitely him," she said, after a moment. "Younger, but I can tell it's him. What's his name?"

"What character is he playing?"

"No bloody idea, I wasn't paying attention."

"Okay, we'll watch it. Sit quiet and listen out for his name."

They watched intently for several minutes.

"Arley. Arley? What kind of a name is that?" Olbeck muttered.

"Skip to the credits," said Kate, almost bouncing in her seat. Olbeck fumbled with the remote.

They watched the credits scroll up the screen. Kate pounced.

"There! Nathan Vertz. We've got it!"

She grabbed her laptop and brought it to life, typing busily into the browser bar.

"Checking IMDB?" asked Olbeck.

Kate nodded. She typed in the name of the film, clicked twice and gave a cry of triumph. She began to read aloud from the screen.

"Nathan Vertz. Former child star of the highly successful *The Butterkins Trilogy*, including *Meet The Butterkins*, *The Butterkins Abroad*, *The Butterkins Christmas*, Nathan Vertz also starred in the independent British production *Wine and Roses*." She looked at Olbeck, awed. "The Butterkins. God, what a blast from the past. Remember those films?"

"I used to love the books." Olbeck looked from the computer screen to the frozen image on the television. "I can't believe that's the same guy who played Toby Butterkin. God."

Kate was busy pulling up more information.

"Look, he's got his own Wikipedia page."

They both regarded the laptop screen. The main picture was of an adorable little boy, his cheeky smile framed by a mop of blonde ringlets.

"You'd never think it was the same person," said Olbeck sadly.

"Nathan Vertz is his real name," said Kate. She traced a finger along the screen. "Born in London... got the part of Toby Butterkin when he was eight. God, that's young. Hmm...hmm...one of the stars of the highly successful franchise... blah, blah... career declined in adulthood...drink and drug dependency..." She looked at Olbeck. "We need to run a check on his name."

"Right. We will. Tomorrow."

Kate paused, halfway to the door.

"What about now?"

"Kate," said Olbeck. "It's almost midnight. It can wait until tomorrow morning."

Kate looked as though she were about to argue. Then she sagged a little.

"Okay. You're right. It's just..."

She let the sentence trail away. Olbeck got up, stretching.

"Jay will be all right, you know," he said, gently. "They'll treat him just as they would anyone else."

"That's what worries me."

Olbeck found his coat and pulled it on, wrapping his scarf around his neck.

"He'll be fine," he repeated. "You can go and see him in the morning. He might even be released before then."

"I know," said Kate. She cleared her throat.

"Thanks, Mark. Thanks for being here tonight. And we found our guy. Imagine that."

"*You* did," said Olbeck. "God, imagine if we'd both been out of the room. He was only a bit character—we could have missed him."

"Well, you picked the DVD," said Kate, with a tired smile. "It must have been fate."

She saw him to the front door. He gave her an awkward hug and said goodbye.

"Try and get some sleep."

Kate nodded. Just as he was turning away, she spoke.

"There's something wrong with this case, Mark."

He turned back, surprised.

"What do you mean?"

"I don't know," said Kate, rather helplessly. "We're missing something, I'm sure of it. Something big. I've never known a case where—oh, I don't know. Where I know something is hidden but all I can see is the surface. Like the river."

"In the picture?" said Olbeck, puzzled.

"Yes. No. I don't know exactly what I'm trying to say."

"That makes two of us."

"It's just...I have a feeling we're missing something, something important." Kate hesitated. She tried to recall where it was she'd felt this most strongly before, but the memory eluded her. "I can't explain it."

"Tell Anderton. Go and see him tomorrow and tell him."

"Tell him what? I don't know what it is myself. Besides—" Kate swallowed, remembering the scene of the afternoon. "He hates me at the moment."

"No, he doesn't." Olbeck yawned. "Listen, I've got to go. Like I said, try and get some sleep. It'll all seem better in the morning."

# Chapter Fourteen

KATE HAD HOPED THAT SHE'D be woken the next morning by the sound of the doorbell. She wanted to open it to find a dishevelled Jay standing on the doorstep, having been released without charge.

She was disappointed.

It was a beautiful sunny morning, warm for late autumn, but she showered and dressed feeling like a grey cloud was hanging over her. The excitement of last night's discovery had ebbed away and now she was dreading seeing Anderton, dreading hearing what had happened with Jay. She wanted to go back to bed, pull the covers over her head and sleep until this nightmare was over. Instead, she squared her shoulders, smoothed back her hair and headed out the door.

Olbeck was already at his desk, looking bright-eyed and bushy-tailed. He waved as he saw Kate come through the door.

"Wait 'til you see this."

Kate slung her coat on the back of her chair.

"I have to go and check on Jay first."

"I've done that. Told him you'd be down to see him."

"Oh, thank you," said Kate, absurdly near tears due to Olbeck's kindness. "I'll go right now."

As it turned out, Jay was asleep in his cell when arrived. She looked through the viewing hatch at her little brother, curled on the uncomfortable bed under the one inadequate grey blanket. He had one hand under his cheek. Kate remembered how he used to sleep like that as a child.

"You want me to wake him up?" asked the PC who was on guard duty.

"No, don't," said Kate, quickly. She looked at her brother with tenderness. "Let him sleep. He needs it. Just tell him I was here when he wakes up."

"All okay?" asked Olbeck when she got back to the office.

Kate shrugged. "Let's not talk about it. Thanks for going down before."

"It's nothing. You're welcome."

"What have you got on Nathan Vertz? Has he got a record?"

Olbeck rolled his chair back from his desk for emphasis.

"Ooh, yes he has."

Kate felt a welcome pulse of excitement,

133

something to distract her from the thought of Jay locked in a cell downstairs. "Really?"

"Yup. See here."

He handed over some print outs. Kate read through the first one and her eyebrows rose.

"Domestic violence. I *see*."

Olbeck was grinning. "Read on. See exactly what he was accused of."

Kate did so. Then she whistled, slowly.

"Attempted strangulation. My God."

"His first wife. Well, his only wife, but she divorced him, unsurprisingly."

Kate read on. "He did six months for that. *That* wasn't on the Wikipedia page."

"Well, that was clearly written by a fan. Anyway, it's not the only time he's been violent. He was arrested for assaulting a member of the paparazzi before the domestic violence charge."

"Back when he was still famous," mused Kate. "How the mighty have fallen. It's sad, really."

"I'll reserve my sympathy for someone who really needs it," said Olbeck. "Anyway, I've brought Anderton up to speed."

Kate couldn't help the drop of her stomach but she managed to hide it at the sound of his name.

"Good," she said. "Let's go and talk to Mr Vertz."

Nathan Vertz lived in Arbuthon Green in a terraced house, one of many on a down-at-heel street. Black bin bags were piled in the street outside every house—it was clearly the day when the dustbin collectors were expected—and several bags had burst or been torn open, scattering rubbish along the street. Kate and Olbeck paused outside the gate of Number 22. The curtains were drawn at all of the visible windows.

"God, when you think about the money he must have had..." said Olbeck, making a face of disgust. He kicked at a soggy newspaper that had wrapped itself around his shoe.

"I know," said Kate. "I think he actually went bankrupt. Come on, let's get him out of bed."

She rang the doorbell repeatedly. When it wasn't answered, she knocked. After a full five minutes, the door opened slowly and Nathan Vertz stood there in the doorway, blinking in the sunlight. A waft of old cigarette smoke and body odour made Kate want to wrinkle up her nose.

"I'm Detective Sergeant Kate Redman, and this is Detective Sergeant Olbeck," she said, snapping her card in his face. He recoiled slightly, shaking his head. "We'd like to talk to you about the murder of Elodie Duncan."

His eyes widened. For a second, Kate was convinced he was going to run—forward between them or backwards into the house—she could see that change of stance, the minute quiver as the impulse flooded his muscles. She tensed, almost as instinctively, ready to chase. She could feel Olbeck do the same. The moment was over and gone in a moment; Nathan Vertz clearly mastered his sudden impulse and some kind of energy went out of him, an almost imperceptible change in his posture. He sighed.

"You'd better come in," he said quietly.

The interior of the house was a surprise. Given the area's general sense of squalor and Nathan Vertz's own grubby appearance, Kate was expecting dirt, frowst, filthy carpets, stale smelling rooms and piles of clutter. Instead, they found rooms that wouldn't have looked out of place in an interiors magazine. The walls were white, the floorboards sanded back and polished. The furniture was old but very well made, some of it clearly valuable. Dotted here and there on the dust-free surfaces were small sculptures, well-framed artwork, a crystal bowl of beautiful autumnal flowers that lit up the corner of the room.

With the backdrop of all this beauty and order, Nathan Vertz presented a strange contrast. His uncut hair fell in greasy spikes on his forehead, although, if she looked closely, Kate could still see the natural curl that had given him the mop of blonde ringlets in the photograph of him as a child.

He sat down on the nearest sofa, an old but sturdy leather Chesterfield, rather like Kate's own.

She felt a secret pride that her own furniture was similar to this man's lovingly collected antiques.

Vertz looked down at the floor. He was sitting slumped, his hands dangling over his knees.

"We're enquiring about the death of Elodie Duncan, Mr Vertz," said Olbeck. "I believe you knew her?"

Vertz said nothing.

"Mr Vertz?"

"I knew her," said Vertz, heavily. "How well, I'm not sure. We went on a few dates."

"Can you elaborate?"

"What do you want me to say?"

"We want you to tell us the truth, Mr Vertz. When you say you went on a few dates, does that mean you were Elodie Duncan's partner? Her boyfriend?"

Vertz was silent.

"Mr Vertz?"

He shook his head.

Olbeck glanced at Kate.

"Mr Vertz," she said sharply. "Obstructing police in the course of their enquiries is a crime. Do you wish to continue this conversation down at the police station?"

Vertz said nothing for a moment. Kate breathed in sharply, ready to start giving the words of the caution. Then he spoke.

"I don't care." He wasn't looking at the officers

but staring at the wall, slumped against the side of the sofa. "I don't care about anything anymore."

Kate and Olbeck exchanged glances. Then they got to their feet.

"We're continuing this conversation back at the station, sir. I suggest you come with us right away."

Vertz was silent on the drive back to the station. Olbeck sat next to him in the back seat. Kate drove, trying not to wrinkle her nose as the man's stale smell permeated the air of the car's interior. Kate looked at him in the rear view mirror. He was staring down at the floor.

She couldn't work him out. He was clearly depressed, but there was something else, something underneath the surface that was making her uneasy. There it was again, that sixth sense, that feeling that she was missing something. Undercurrent: that was the word she was looking for.

She let Olbeck take him to one of the interview rooms, one of the less-pleasant ones on the ground floor. Then she ran down to the holding cells.

Jay had been released. Kate had expected to feel jubilant at the news—that must mean that they hadn't found any more evidence with which to hold him, or God forbid, to charge him. But instead, she felt worry begin to gnaw at her, cramping her stomach. Her brother was young. He was struggling over the death of his friend; he'd just been through the trauma of an arrest and a night's imprisonment, not to mention the intimidating questioning session he would have gone through with Anderton and Jerry. Would he be all right? She tried to call him, his mobile going straight to voicemail. Then she called her mother—same thing. Eventually, Kate managed to get through to Courtney, who said she'd keep trying until she got through to him. Kate thanked her, told her she loved her, and hung up, running frantically up the stairs to the interview room before smoothing her hair down, trying to get her breath back and opening the door.

# Chapter Fifteen

"DS REDMAN HAS ENTERED THE room," said Olbeck, also giving the time.

Kate sat down opposite Nathan Vertz. He gave her a dull look, almost bovine in its weariness, before resuming his apparent examination of the table-top.

"Mr Vertz, you have been seen with Elodie Duncan on more than one occasion." Olbeck was clearly still referring to the suspect as a 'Mister.' How soon this changed would depend on the responses he was given. Kate was less patient and often dispensed with the title in the first few moments.

Olbeck continued.

"Several witnesses have confirmed that you were with Elodie on the night that she died. I will ask you again: did you have anything to do with her death?"

"No."

"Can you confirm the time and place you last saw Elodie on the night of the eighth of November?"

"No comment."

"What do you think happened?"

There was a flicker on Vertz's set face. "I don't know."

Olbeck sat back in his seat, clearly suppressing his irritation. He looked over at Kate, giving her tacit permission to take over.

Kate sat up, pulled her shirt sleeves down straight over her wrists and put her shoulders back.

"Are you musical, Mr Vertz?"

This was clearly not the question he'd been expecting. He gave her a glance of surprise, the first sign of animation she'd seen.

"I was, once." He pushed the hair out of his eyes with the back of his hand. "I was a good singer, once."

Kate recalled something about the Butterkins films—hadn't they been adapted for the stage as well?

"That's something that you and Elodie had in common," she said. "She was very talented musically."

He was looking at her properly now, as if she'd suddenly come into focus.

"She was. She was amazing."

"Did she ever play for you?"

Vertz actually smiled. Dirty as he was, unsavoury as he was, Kate could suddenly see his appeal for Elodie: the smile made him look eager, boyish, and vulnerable in an attractive way.

"She did, many times."

Kate contrasted that remark with Vertz's previous assertion that he and Elodie had been 'on a few dates.'

"So you did actually spend quite a lot of time together?"

Vertz looked uncomfortable. "I suppose so."

"Did you ever meet her family?"

"No."

"Did she ever talk to you about her family at all? Did she mention her relationship with her parents?"

A flash in Vertz's eyes but he shook his head.

"No."

"Did you meet Elodie's friends?"

"No."

"None of them? Amy Peters?"

"No."

Kate cleared her throat.

"What about Jason Redman?"

"No." Vertz was sounding bored.

Kate sat back. It was Olbeck's turn.

He didn't disappoint her.

"Elodie Duncan was in possession of a large amount of cocaine, Mr Vertz. Do you know anything about this?"

Vertz didn't react. "No comment."

"Did you give it to her?"

"No comment."

"You have numerous convictions for drug related offences, Nathan." Ah, there. He'd lost the Mister. Kate was surprised it had taken this long.

"Your girlfriend—your dead girlfriend—had drugs in her possession. Are you expecting me to believe there was no connection between these two facts?"

Vertz stared out of the tiny window, set high up in the wall.

"No comment."

They kept it up for another hour, digging away, trying to find a weak spot. Vertz ignored the questions, or answered negatively, or replied 'no comment.' The only time Vertz showed any sign of animation was when Elodie's talent for music was highlighted.

Eventually, they had to let him go.

"Bugger," said Olbeck as they watched Nathan walk away from the station with his head down.

"We should have charged him" said Kate. "Kept him in." After all, Anderton had done just that to Jay, hadn't he? How was that fair? "He knows more than he's saying."

Olbeck gave her an old-fashioned look. "Well, of course he does. He's guilty as sin in my opinion."

"So why didn't we bloody charge him?" Kate snapped. She turned on her heel and walked back to her desk, pulling out her chair with an irritable tug.

"Temper," said Olbeck, sitting back down. "And actually, I agree with you. I'm going to update Anderton and see what he wants to do."

"Fine. Do that."

Kate reached for the phone as soon as he'd walked away and dialled the coroner's office.

"Doctor Telling? It's Kate Redman—fine, thanks. How was your holiday?"

She leant back, tapping a pencil on her jaw. Doctor Telling had a very quiet, measured voice, the sort where you instinctively relaxed listening to it. Kate had always thought that if the pathology thing didn't work out, the good doctor had an excellent career ahead of her as a voiceover artist for relaxation and meditation tracks.

"Sorry, I didn't quite catch that—the *Arctic*? Oh, a cruise. Well that's sounds...yes. Did Doctor Stanton tell you what we wanted? Oh you have—brilliant. Yes, I'm sorry, we only got one of the samples very recently, today in fact. Sorry—yes, please. No, I'll wait."

She held the receiver to her ear as Doctor Telling made rummaging and mouse-clicking noises on the other end of the line. Then that quiet, comforting voice came back on the line.

Kate's eyebrows rose.

"Seriously? That's great. Yes, if you could send over the info, we'd be really grateful. Thanks so much."

Kate put the receiver down, obscurely comforted that Doctor Telling had been somewhere suitably weird for her holiday. She threw her pen over at Olbeck, who had just come back to his desk.

"The DNA results are back. Telling's sending them over now."

"So," said Olbeck. "Don't keep me in suspense. Who's the daddy?"


WHEN KATE ARRIVED HOME THAT night, she found two waifs and strays on her doorstep—Courtney and Jay. They were sat side by side, huddled in their coats and smoking cigarettes. The area around their feet was littered with cigarette butts.

"You must be freezing," exclaimed Kate. She opened up the door and ushered them both in. How long had they been sitting out there? "How long have you been sitting out there?"

"Fucking ages," muttered Courtney. She was hunched over by the kitchen counter, her hands in her armpits. Her beautiful, sulky face was pinched, her nose and cheeks reddened by the cold.

Jay stood silently. Kate gave him a quick hug, feeling the sharp bones of his ribcage under her hands. She stood back and took him by the arms, looking into his face.

"It'll be all right, Jay," she said gently. "They haven't charged you with anything. It'll be all right."

He looked at her quickly and then away. For a moment she thought he was going to say something, and then he shook his head, gently detached her hands and walked away.

"There's just one thing," Kate said awkwardly. "You can't stay here. I'm really sorry, but I don't think it would be appropriate." She paused, hating the sound of her voice and her mealy-mouthed words. "I think you'd be better off somewhere where people don't know where to find you."

Jay laughed harshly.

"That's my digs out then. I'm not going back there anyway. I don't want everyone looking at me and thinking I did it."

Kate put both hands to her head and rubbed her temples. She was so tired: her eyes ached, her back ached, her feet ached.

"How about I drop you at Mum's? You can stay there for a while."

Courtney looked as though she was about to protest. Kate looked over at her sister. "Is that a bad idea? What about your dad?"

Courtney shook her head. "He's up in Scotland. Has been for ages."

"Oh. It'll have to be Mum's place, then. She won't mind." Kate hoped fervently that this were true. "Stay here tonight—both of you stay—and I'll run you both back tomorrow before work."

She ran a bath for Jay, found something to watch on television for Courtney, and put a couple of frozen pizzas in the oven. They ate the pizzas in a fairly companionable silence, and then the two youngsters disappeared out the back to smoke a last cigarette before bed. Kate bundled herself up in her coat and swept up all the butts from outside her front door. She put aside the uncharitable thought that if they had money for cigarettes, why on Earth did they always plead such poverty?

When she came back inside, Jay had already gone to bed. Courtney was glued to her phone screen with the television playing unheeded in the background.

"Well, I'm off to bed," said Kate. "Do you want to bunk in with me or would you rather have the sofa?"

"Sofa, sis, ta."

Kate fetched the remaining spare duvet and a pillow. Courtney stood up while Kate made up the sofa with the bedding. While she was smoothing out the pillow case, she could feel Courtney fidgeting behind her. She turned and raised her eyebrows.

"You okay?"

"Yeah," said Courtney. She seemed about to say more, but then her mobile pinged and she turned her attention back to the screen.

Kate hesitated for a moment. She had a feeling that Courtney had wanted to ask her something or tell her something.

"Courtney? Are you—is there something wrong?"

Courtney actually looked up from her phone. She looked frightened for a moment. Then she shook her head.

Kate stood, irresolute. Then she yawned and gave up. She was just too tired to get to the bottom of whatever it was—and it probably wasn't even important.

She yawned again and said goodnight.

# Chapter Sixteen

IT WAS A SILENT DRIVE on the way to Mary Redman's house the next morning. As Kate drove past her mother's place, looking for a parking space, she saw a bright yellow Mini parked on the scrubby front lawn.

"Is Peter living here now?"

"Yeah," said Courtney.

Kate pulled the car into the kerb.

"Must be a bit crowded. With you two girls here as well." Courtney had been living with her father but clearly had decided a room at her mother's place was preferable to moving to Scotland.

Courtney shrugged. She looked at Kate, opened her mouth and then shut it again.

"What—" Kate was interrupted by Jay getting out of the car and slamming the door shut.

As they walked up the front path, past the Mini, the dirty net curtains at the front window flickered. Peter's face peered out, and momentarily, a frown crossed his face. The curtains were pulled across again, hiding his face from view. By that time, though, Kate had already processed that look.

When Kate had been a 'bobby on the beat,' very early on in her career, she'd been out with her Sergeant, a bluff Northerner called Wittock. He'd told her about what he'd termed 'coppers' senses': something almost indefinable that every good police officer developed. It was almost a sixth sense: the ability to deduct that something was awry from the smallest of gestures or inconsequential details.

"It takes time," Wittock had said. "But you'll get it. If you're any good at your job. You'll start to notice things, without even realising you're noticing them, if you see what I mean."

Kate had found he was right. And now, just on that one look from Peter, a momentary expression on his face seen in the fraction of a second, her copper's senses were screaming.

When he opened the door, he was all smiles and solicitous attention for Jay, ushering them all inside with warm greetings.

"Mary's out shopping," he said, gesturing for them to go through into the living room. It was much cleaner and tidier than it had been last time Kate had been here, although the stink of old cigarettes had not noticeably lessened. "Jade's at school, obviously. How are you, Kate?"

"Fine, thanks," said Kate, keeping a smile on her face. Jay sloped past them and she heard him walking heavily up the stairs. Courtney followed him a moment later.

"How about a cup of tea?"

"Lovely," said Kate, automatically. She'd noticed a laptop on the coffee table, the screen facing away from the room.

Peter followed her gaze.

"Just doing my accounts," he said. "Worst thing about being self-employed, the bloomin' paperwork!"

"I can imagine."

"I'll get you that tea. Sit down love, and I won't be long."

"Thanks," said Kate, her cheeks beginning to ache from smiling. Peter went off to the galley kitchen at the end of the hallway, leaving the door open behind him.

"Milk and sugar?" he shouted from the kitchen.

"Just milk, please," Kate shouted back. Quickly and quietly, she walked to the laptop so she could see the screen and gently tapped the spacebar to take off the screensaver. She was expecting a password request to come up, but there was nothing. There was nothing on the screen except the usual Outlook interface, emails and a little calendar. Nothing untoward.

Kate quickly ran her eye down the list of emails. Only one caught her attention and that was because the subject matter was a girl's name: Alice. She opened it, glancing towards the open door. What on Earth was she going to say if Peter came back and caught her? The email opened. Kate scanned it quickly.

> **From:** gil450231@gmail.com
> **To:** pbuckley@hotmail.co.uk
> **Subject:** Alice
> **Message:** got those files you were looking for. Check new website https://www.nys1016.com.

Nothing untoward there either. Kate tried to memorise the address and then whipped out her mobile and took a photograph of the screen. She could hear the kettle in the kitchen come to the boil. Quickly, she closed the email to bring back the original screen, tiptoed back to the sofa and sat down, checking the photograph had saved correctly. Then she put her phone away, just as Peter appeared in the doorway with two steaming mugs.

They made chit-chat while Kate tried to drink her hot tea as quickly as she decently could. Then she said goodbye to Peter, hugged Courtney and Jay who were listening to music and smoking cigarettes in Courtney's bedroom, and told them both to give her love to her Mum.

"Where've you bloody *been*?" said Olbeck as Kate dropped into her chair at the office. "We've pulled Nathan Vertz in again, under caution this time."

"Good," said Kate. "Are we questioning him?"

"Nope, Anderton's doing it. We've been sent over to Vertz's place to pull it apart. We'll take Jane and Rav as well if they're free."

The four of them drove in two separate cars to Arbuthon Green. It was intensely cold: the first real frost of the season. The grubby terraces were almost transformed, glittering under a powdery dusting of ice.

Nathan Vertz's house was warm and clean and quiet.

"Wow, nice," said Jane, looking around with eyebrows raised. "You'd never think he had a place like this."

"I know," said Kate. She rubbed a finger along her jaw, wondering whether to say what she wanted to say. "I think—"

"Hey, look at this," said Rav, who was opening cupboards. "Awards. Not for the *Butterkins*, surely?"

"Don't be such a snob," said Olbeck. "They were really popular once. Made millions for the British film industry."

"Well, what happened to it all? Vertz's share, I mean." Rav took an award out of the cupboard, turning it over in his gloved hands. "*People's*

153

*Choice*." He glanced at Olbeck. "See, it's hardly an Oscar, is it?"

Kate and Jane took the upstairs rooms, leaving the men to cover the ground floor. Nathan Vertz's bedroom was as beautifully decorated as the rest of the house; the walls were painted a pale, chalky green, the large bed made up with white linen. The duvet and pillows were rumpled and dragged half onto the floor. There was a small, delicate little wooden table by the bed, a lamp with a fawn silk shade still switched on. Kate turned it off. She pulled out the drawer of the bedside table. Inside was a collection of letters and postcards. Kate drew them out and sat on the edge of the messy bed to read through them. Beneath her feet was the scrape of something heavy being moved as the men began to shift the furniture.

"Look," she said to Jane after a moment. The other woman came over and Kate handed her the topmost letter.

"It's from Elodie."

Jane read silently for a moment. Then she looked at Kate.

"A love letter."

Kate fanned out the rest of the papers in her hands. "Lots of love letters. I didn't think anyone wrote love letters any more."

Jane took another one, a postcard of a Turner

landscape. She read the inscription on the back out loud.

"'Remembering that afternoon in the cornfields. I love you.'" She turned it over and looked at the picture of the front, flipped it back again. "It's dated...August this year."

Kate pulled the drawer completely out and looked through it.

"There's nothing there from him to her," said Jane, sorting through the stack of correspondence.

"Well, would there be?"

"I guess not. Were there any letters from Vertz at Elodie's house when you searched it?"

Kate sat back on her haunches and stared at Jane. "No. No, there wasn't. Not a single thing."

"Well," said Jane, hesitatingly. "That's odd—isn't it?"

"Yes, it is," said Kate. She pulled herself to her feet with a groan. "I mean, he could be the sort of guy who doesn't ever write letters but...it's a bit odd."

She scanned the letters. "Look, here. She says, 'Thanks for your beautiful letter.' So he must have written at least one."

Jane opened her mouth to reply but before she could say anything, there was a shout from downstairs.

Kate and Jane arrived in the living room to see

the sofa pushed back against the wall, the rug rolled up and a section of the floorboards upended.

Rav was grinning like a child who had just discovered a playmate during a game of hide and seek.

"The motherlode."

Kate looked down into the space beneath the floorboards revealed by the upended wood. Several plastic-wrapped packages, a scuffed black rucksack, a half-empty sack of glucose powder, a set of scales.

"Well, well," said Olbeck. "At least one part of the mystery is cleared up." He carefully opened the rucksack with gloved hands without moving it from its original position. "Look here. Must be..." He riffled through the wads of neatly bound bank notes in the bag. "Must be thousands here."

Jane was already on the radio arranging for crime scene photographers. Kate, who was nearest the front window, noticed several cars drawing up outside the house. For a second, she thought it was some of their own officers before the cameras appearing put paid to that idea.

"Press are here," she said.

Jane rolled her eyes. "That didn't take long."

"We'd better get some uniforms here, cordon it off."

Kate drew the curtains across the windows. Rav was already phoning for reinforcements.

Olbeck drew Kate aside.

"Let's get back to Anderton, let him have the latest. This could be the trigger he's been waiting for."

# Chapter Seventeen

ANDERTON WAS QUESTIONING VERTZ IN one of the interview rooms when Olbeck and Kate arrived back at the station. Nathan Vertz looked even more dishevelled than he had done the day before, eyes ringed by shadow, his face pale and pouchy. Kate and Olbeck waited outside while Anderton paused the interview and left the room, joining them in the corridor.

"What have you got for me?"

They told him. Kate was thankful she was able to be calm and professional. It meant the embarrassment of being in Anderton's company after their last disastrous meeting was somewhat mitigated.

All three went back into the interview room and Kate was sure that, this time, Anderton would take no prisoners. She kept the folder containing Elodie's letters on her lap, ready to hand it over at the right time.

Vertz flicked a single glance at her as she sat

down before lapsing back into blankness. Again, she had the impression that there was something there under the surface, something hidden but dangerous. She'd felt it before, with someone else, someone quite different to this unshaven, slouched man before her. Who had it been?

She thought back and realised it was Mrs Duncan, Elodie's mother. Some other feeling had been there under the grief, barely glimpsed, like the tiniest tip of an iceberg poking out from chilly, black waters.

"So, Nathan," said Anderton quietly. "You maintain that the extent of your relationship with Elodie Duncan is that 'you went on a few dates.' Do you wish to amend that statement?"

Vertz said nothing but kept staring at the table top.

"I put it to you that you had a longstanding and deep romantic and sexual relationship with Elodie Duncan."

Silence from Vertz.

"Can you confirm if that is the case?"

Vertz continued to stare at the table top.

No one spoke for a few moments. Then Anderton took up the gauntlet again.

"A large quantity of cocaine was found in Elodie Duncan's possession after she died. My officers have just informed me that an even larger quantity of cocaine and other assorted illegal substances was found hidden away at your house today. Do you have anything to say about that?"

Nothing. Kate suppressed an irritated sigh. Stonewalling during an interview was an effective technique but surely there was something they could do to break him down... She pressed the side of her foot against Anderton's under the table and passed him the folder of love letters.

He didn't break stride in what he was saying but took the folder from her, continuing to ask Nathan Vertz his questions.

"Did you give that cocaine to Elodie Duncan for her to sell for you?"

"No comment," muttered Vertz. The solicitor beside him shifted uneasily.

"Did Elodie try to rip you off? Did you kill her?"

"No she didn't. And no I didn't."

"Who do you think killed her?"

There was a sudden stillness in Vertz. Kate was reminded of an animal that had just scented its prey. Or was it an animal who had just heard the hunter stalking it?

"I don't know," he said in a quiet voice. There was something hidden in his statement that made Kate want to shiver.

Anderton let the silence after his remark continue for an uncomfortably long time. Then he slowly held up one of Elodie's letters and began to read from it aloud.

"'My darling Nathan, can't wait to see you again tonight. I know we only said goodbye a few days ago but it just seems too long before we can be together again. It's only when I'm with you that I really feel like myself—'"

Vertz went pale.

"Where did you get that?"

Anderton ignored him. He let the letter fall to his lap and picked up a postcard.

"'Hey, my sexy Nat, saw this and thought of you—'"

Vertz snatched for it, and Anderton pulled his hand back.

"That's mine!"

Vertz was on his feet. Kate and Olbeck leapt to theirs, and the uniformed officer in the corner did likewise. The solicitor, a grey-haired man in his sixties, looked as though he was ready to run out of the door.

Anderton hadn't moved. Without taking his eyes from Vertz's face, he slowly drew another postcard and held it, preparing to read from it.

"Stop."

Vertz's voice broke in a sob. Suddenly, he flopped back onto his chair, burying his face in his hands.

After a moment, Anderton spoke quietly.

"You loved Elodie Duncan, didn't you Nathan?"

Vertz was crying, harsh, open-mouthed sobs. The tears were running between his dirty fingers.

161

Anderton repeated his statement.

"You loved her, didn't you Nathan?"

Vertz nodded. After a moment, he spoke, his voice hoarse.

"I loved her. We—we found each other—we knew each other. We both knew what it was like..." His voice trailed away into a mumble. Then he cleared his throat and spoke again. "I didn't kill her. I would never hurt her."

"You have a police record for assaulting your wife," said Anderton. "A serious assault. Are you telling me you've changed that much?"

"That was different. Elodie was different."

"What happened that night?"

Vertz shook his head. "I don't know. I don't know."

"Did you kill Elodie Duncan?"

"No, I didn't. I would never hurt her." He began to cry again. "I wouldn't do that."

Anderton placed the letters back into the folder, gently. He closed it and gave it back to Kate. Vertz tracked the movement with his eyes.

"Those are mine."

"You will have them back, Nathan," said Anderton. Then he said, in the same gentle voice, "Are you aware that Elodie was pregnant when she died?"

If Vertz had been pale before, it was nothing to the colour he became. He looked almost transparent.

"What?" he whispered.

"Elodie Duncan was pregnant when she died," said Anderton, looking straight at the man. Some premonition made Kate brace herself, shift herself just a little closer to the edge of her seat.

Anderton continued.

"It was your baby."

Vertz exploded. Roaring, he flung himself forward, shouting something incomprehensible. Anderton and Kate dived, one to each side, and then Olbeck was on Vertz, the officer flinging himself forward, shouting for reinforcements. Anderton pushed Kate towards the door as the uniformed officers stampeded into the room, piling themselves on the struggling Vertz. His wordless shouts resolved themselves into a recognisable word.

"*No, no, no...*"

He continued to scream as they dragged him from the room. Kate could hear him as he was pulled towards the cells, getting fainter with every step.

His cries were abruptly cut off as the heavy metal door to the cells swung closed with a crash. The silence left behind seemed deafening.

Anderton still had his hand on Kate's arm. They both looked at it as if suddenly remembering it was there. Anderton removed it quickly.

"You all right?" he asked.

Kate nodded. She was still trembling slightly from the backwash of adrenaline.

"He wasn't expecting that," she said.

"No, he wasn't," Anderton agreed. He pushed his hands through this hair and dropped them to his sides, exhaling loudly. "There'll be no more out of him tonight. He won't be in any fit state."

Kate nodded. She knew that Vertz was probably being sedated right about now. She took a deep breath. Her trembling gradually stopped, but she felt empty, hollow, and suddenly depressed.

"Fancy a drink?" said Anderton suddenly.

Kate looked at him in surprise, so shocked she didn't at first know how to answer.

"Now?" she managed, after a moment.

"Yes, right now."

She was still so surprised she agreed without thinking.

Once they were in the pub and sat down with their drinks, the awkwardness between them threatened to return. Kate cast about for something to say, something to break the conversational deadlock, but she couldn't think of anything that didn't have some sort of negative connotation. She took a hurried sip of her orange juice.

"Do you ever drink?" asked Anderton abruptly. "Alcohol, I mean."

Kate shrugged. "Sometimes. At Christmas. It's just not my thing."

"Why is that?"

"Does there have to be a reason?"

"There normally is."

Kate sighed. "My mum's a drinker. Not exactly an alcoholic but—well, perhaps she is an alcoholic. I don't really know. She drinks too much, anyway." Talking of her mother reminded her of Peter and the email she'd discovered. She must look into that when she got home later. "It's just not something I enjoy, I'm afraid."

"Don't apologise." Anderton turned his pint glass around a few times. "You'll probably outlive us all." He looked up into her eyes. "Or perhaps you've got plenty of other secret vices."

Kate smiled in order to hide the sudden physical jolt his words had given her. "I do have a secret fondness for *Gardener's World*."

Anderton actually laughed. Then the smile from his face dropped abruptly and another awkward silence fell.

"Sir," said Kate after a moment, rather hesitatingly. She wasn't exactly sure what she wanted to say. "This case—"

"What about it?"

Kate sat up a little straighter. Then she shook her head. "I'm sorry, I don't know what I'm trying to say. I'm confused."

"Please tell me you're not hiding anything else from me that I need to know."

"No," said Kate, shocked and a little hurt. "All I mean is—oh, I don't know. There's something more to this case than what we're seeing, what we're investigating. Can't you feel it too, sir? There's something underneath it all that we haven't got yet."

Anderton was regarding her intently. "I think I know what you mean."

Kate dropped her head momentarily into her hands. When she raised it, she looked Anderton directly in the eye.

"There's so much *rage* in this case," she murmured. "Everyone connected with Elodie is just so angry. Vertz. Her mother. Her stepfather. There's this constant, simmering undercurrent of anger everywhere."

"Yes, there is."

Anderton suddenly sounded exhausted. There was another beat of silence. Kate was about to speak again when he pre-empted her.

"I owe you an apology, Kate."

Kate went blank for a moment.

"You do?" she said.

"Yes. I was totally wrong to speak to you like I did the other day. It was extremely unprofessional of me, and for that I sincerely apologise."

Kate muttered, "That's all right." What else could she say?

Anderton leaned forward a little.

"I'm not used to apologising," he said. "'Never apologise, never explain.' That was always my motto."

"Everyone thinks it was Churchill who said that," said Kate. "But it was actually some Victorian admiral, I can't remember his name."

Anderton grinned. "I'll let you off. Anyway, things...circumstances change. I'm sorry."

"It's fine," said Kate, a little awkwardly. "I should have come to see you first of all, anyway. It was my fault as—as much as yours."

Silence returned but this time it was easier. They had nearly reached the end of the drinks, and Kate opened her mouth to ask if he wanted another. Again, he pre-empted her.

"My marriage is breaking down," he said. Kate was again so surprised she was struck dumb. Anderton went on. "Well, breaking down is too positive. It's broken. It's over."

"I'm sorry."

Anderton leant back in his chair, staring up at the ceiling.

"When you came into my office the other day, I'd just finished a call to my soon-to-be-ex wife. I was barely thinking straight, I was so upset. And then you came in and told me something that, ordinarily, would just merit a brief ticking off. It seemed like the last straw, just then. I blew up—"

CELINA GRACE

"I know," said Kate. "I was there."

Anderton gave her a tired smile. "You chose the worst possible moment and bore the brunt of it. I'm sorry."

Their eyes met again, and Kate was again aware of something she'd been forcing down for so long that she'd almost forgotten it was there. Her attraction, her desire for Anderton crystallised in one long, charged moment. What made it worse was that she knew he was suddenly aware of it too. There was a breathless pause in which all the hubbub surrounding them faded away and there was just the two of them, eyes locked, leaning towards each other over the table.

Anderton put a hand over hers.

"Kate—"

Kate shot to her feet, knocking over her glass, dislodging his hand.

"Just going to the loo—back in a moment."

She hurried down the stairs to the toilets in the basement of the pub, almost falling in her haste to get away from him. She locked herself in a cubicle and sat on the closed seat for a moment, her hands over her eyes. *He's married, he's your boss; don't go there. He's married, he's your boss; don't go there.* She was shaken with the intensity of her desire, by the raw, urgent hunger she felt for him. *He's married, even if it's over. He's your boss. Just get up, go back, smile, say goodbye, and leave.*

168

As it turned out, she needn't have worried. When she got back to the table, Olbeck and Jerry were there, deep in conversation with Anderton. He looked up briefly as she came back and smiled, a quick flicker meant solely for her. Kate sat down, grateful for the company of the others.

For the rest of the evening, she barely said a word.

# Chapter Eighteen

THERE WAS NO WAY THAT anyone would be questioning Nathan Vertz the next morning. Kate had been informed that when the doctor's sedative had worn off, Vertz had launched a bleary attack on his cell door: kicking it, shouting, rebounding off the frame to stumble to his knees. The doctor had been called again and had examined him, announcing that no interrogation would be possible for some time. Two representatives from the Mental Health Team were called and spent several hours with Vertz in his cell. Anderton had him under twenty-four-hour observation. Kate knew as well as Anderton that if a vulnerable suspect wanted to kill themselves, they would do their best to find a way.

"I've not lost one on my watch yet, and I'm not about to start now," Anderton said, striding ahead of Kate down the corridor back to the office. "We've got another day, and then we'll have to charge him or let him go again."

"I know," puffed Kate, hurrying to keep up. She

wondered whether she'd mistaken that electric moment between the two of them the night before. Thank God she hadn't done anything about it. Best to put it to the back of her mind once more and focus all her energies on the job.

This good intention buoyed her up for all of five minutes once she sat down at her desk. She was very tired after a restless night with bad dreams and fractured sleep. She made herself a strong coffee, rubbed her eyes, and sat down to bury herself in paperwork. For once, she was glad of Olbeck sitting across from her and moaning softly that his head was killing him. He still found time to respond to whomever it was that kept sending him text messages, sending his phone buzzing and skittering across the desk like a large, shiny insect.

"Would you turn that off?" snapped Kate eventually, unable to take any more.

Olbeck gave her a hurt look. Kate pinched the bridge of her nose and tried to concentrate. Something was nagging at the back of her mind. Something about a phone message. She stared mindlessly into space for five minutes before she remembered.

She took out her own phone and hunted through the applications until she came to her photograph storage. There was the one she'd taken of the screen of Peter Buckley's laptop, the picture of the email that had piqued her curiosity.

> **From:** gil450231@gmail.com
> **To:** pbuckley@hotmail.co.uk
> **Subject:** Alice
> **Message:** got those files you were looking for. Check new website https://www.nys1016.com.

Kate brought up an internet browser on her computer and typed in the website address. A blank blue screen came up with a password-protected log-in box in the middle. Kate frowned. She tried typing in Peter's name and 'password,' then his email address and 'password.' Error messages came up. She sat back, blowing out her cheeks. There was no way she was going to be able to guess his password, and she didn't know whether the site would automatically log her out after a certain number of erroneous attempts. She tapped her pen against her jaw for a moment and then picked up the phone.

"I'm heading down to IT," she said to Olbeck after a short telephone conversation. He grunted, finally intent on his work.

"Hi Sam," said Kate to Sam Hollington, the youngest, newest and keenest member of the

Abbeyford team's Information and Technology Department.

"Hi Kate. What've you got for me?"

Sam had a round face, round wire-framed spectacles, and a mop of curly black hair. He reminded Kate of a Labrador puppy, in the nicest possible way.

"Can you check out a website for me? Who owns it, who the domain is registered to—anything, really."

"No probs. Gimme the URL and leave it with me."

Kate resisted the urge to pat him on the head. "You're a star. Thanks Sam."

"When do you need it?"

Kate paused, her hand on the door handle.

"No real hurry," she said. "It's probably not important. Whenever you can do it."

"Righto."

Checking her watch as she reached the ground floor—IT was located in the depths of the basement—Kate could see it was nearly one o'clock. Lunchtime. She hesitated, debating whether to drag Olbeck to the canteen or head outside to grab some fresh air and a sandwich. The lure of the outside won. She pushed the door open to the station foyer and immediately spotted Jay and Courtney, waiting side by side on the uncomfortable chairs against the wall. Both of them looked scared and small and young.

Kate reached them in three large strides. They both stood up together and the three of them stood in an odd little huddle for a moment.

Kate put both of her hands on their arms, one on each.

"What's wrong?"

Jay swallowed. His face was noticeably thinner, his eyes ringed with shadow.

"I've come to change my statement," he said.

The floor rocked for a moment. Kate closed her eyes and opened them again.

Courtney put her hand into Kate's, much as she had when she was a little girl.

"Sis—"

"Why—why now, Jay?" whispered Kate. She had a sudden, piercing flash of memory: baby Jay in her mother's arms, smiling gummily up at his big sister, clamping his tiny fingers around Kate's thumb. He used to grab onto her fingers while she was feeding him and pull her hand up and down as he sucked at the bottle, surprisingly strong for a baby. She fought the urge to turn him around bodily and push him back out the door into the street, before it was too late.

"I have to, sis," he said. He was deathly pale, but his chin was up, his shoulders squared. Kate knew she couldn't stop him. She stepped back, Courtney's hand slipping from hers.

Kate handed Jay over to Theo and watched as the two men walked away along the corridor to the interview rooms. Her ears buzzed. What was Jay going to say? What was he going to confess to? A bubble of nausea came up into her throat.

Courtney was still standing beside her, almost hanging onto her arm. Kate turned to her little sister.

"Do you—do you know this is about?"

Courtney, her eyes huge, her mouth pinched, nodded.

Kate swallowed. "I can't talk to you right now, Courtney. Don't wait. You should go home."

Courtney shook her head.

"I want to wait for Jay."

How could Kate tell her that she might wait all night, all the next day? How could she tell her that he might not be released at all?

She put her hands on Courtney's shoulders.

"Don't wait here, darling. It might take—it might take a long time. Why not go home?"

"I don't want to."

"All right," Kate said helplessly. "How about I give you some money and you find yourself a coffee shop or something? Have a look around the shops?"

For a second she thought Courtney was going to

argue with her. Then the younger woman's eyes fell and she nodded.

"Okay."

Kate pulled her into a quick hug.

"Give me a sec," she said, her mouth against Courtney's messy hair. "Let me get my purse. I won't be long."

She ran along the corridor and up the stairs, not waiting for the lifts. What room had Jay been taken to? At her desk, Kate grabbed her handbag and riffled through it for her purse. The phone on her desk rang.

She hesitated. For a moment, she was determined not to answer it. Then duty got the better of her and she snatched it up.

"Kate Redman."

"Kate, it's Sam." For a second, she had to think about who that was. Because of her state of mind, it took her a moment to recognise his voice.

"Sam, I'm kind of busy right now—"

"It's about that website you asked me to look at." Now she could hear the shock in his voice. "I think you need to see it."

"Oh God—" Kate squeezed her eyes shut for a second. "Can't it wait?"

"I think you need to see it."

Kate breathed out as slowly as she could, tamping down a scream of frustration. It wasn't Sam's fault, after all.

"Okay," she said, after a moment. "I'm on my way."

She pounded back to the foyer, tucked a tenner in Courtney's hand and kissed her. "Now, don't *worry*," she emphasised, gently propelling her sister out of the station entrance. "Come back in a few hours. Text me and I'll come down and meet you."

Courtney gave her a wan smile and trotted obediently down the station steps at the entrance. Kate watched her cross the road and waved when she turned back for a last look before disappearing around the corner. Then Kate swivelled on her heel and ran back across the foyer, heading for the steps to the basement. She had to physically force herself past the turn off to the interview rooms. What in God's name was Jay confessing to in there?

Sam met her at the door to the IT department. His round, friendly face was pale, his freckles standing out.

"What is it?" asked Kate, trying not to sound as impatient as she felt.

He said nothing but beckoned her towards his desk. His monitor was showing a screensaver of a poster from the film *Watchmen*.

"I know you didn't ask me to hack into it," Sam said, bent over his desk and keying in what was obviously his password. "But I thought I'd give it a go. Anyway—"

"You can do that?" Kate said, moving closer.

Sam gave her a worried grin from over his shoulder. "Yeah, of course. But anyway, I wish I hadn't." He straightened up and looked around to see if anyone was near them. "Look."

He moved away from the screen. Kate heard herself grunt, an involuntary noise of shock. Hand to her mouth, she took in the images on the screen. Nice Young Sluts! screamed the header. Kate's gaze moved from one girl to the other. Incredibly, some were smiling, or at least their teeth were bared. Most were not.

"Oh my God."

Sam and Kate exchanged a glance of shared horror. Then Kate put her hand over her eyes.

"Put the screen saver on again. Please."

Sam tapped keys. Kate sat down heavily in his seat.

"Did you find out who it's registered to?" she said, after a moment of catching her breath.

"Of course. That's the first thing I did. The WHOIS was cloaked, but I soon got past that." He took a sheet of paper from his in-tray. "It's all on there. There you are. Registered to a G. Lightbody. The sick bugger."

Kate grabbed the paper from him and tried to hold it steady in her shaking hand. There it was, in black and white. She stared at the name and then past it, seeing nothing, her mind whirring. There was a moment of blackness, of staring into the void, and then a massive flare of light, comprehension exploding in a burst of sparks. She actually saw it, like fireworks in her mind.

"What should I do?" said Sam. "I'm kind of freaked out by that being on my computer."

Kate leapt up.

"Get everything you can on it," she said, already moving away. "Screenshots, print outs, anything. Whatever trail you can find from that site. IP addresses, any emails, *anything*. Get everyone onto it."

"Really?" said Sam. "Everyone?"

"Everyone. Thanks Sam. Got to go!"

She was already running by the time she got to the door. She leapt up the stairs, paused for a quick scan of the foyer—no sign of Courtney—before running up to the office. Olbeck was there, just putting on his coat.

"Come with me," gasped Kate, so breathless she could barely form the words.

"Where are we going?"

She grabbed his arm and pulled.

"Anderton's office. Right now."

# Chapter Nineteen

AT NINE O'CLOCK THAT NIGHT, Kate was slumped on her sofa with Courtney, the two of them digesting a greasy Chinese takeaway. Watching television, she had the surreal experience of seeing herself on the news. It had happened a couple of times before, but she still hadn't got used to it. There she was, flanking Graham Lightbody as he was escorted from the grounds of Rawlwood College. Anderton loomed on the other side of him. Lightbody was a small man, but he looked even more shrunken on the screen. He'd been trembling as they walked away towards the police car.

Kate could see her own face on the screen, just briefly in the shot as she got into the car after their suspect; she was frowning and trying not to. She wondered whether the viewers of the local news would notice. Would they realise it was because she was concentrating hard on not punching Graham Lightbody in the face?

"Look, it's you," exclaimed Courtney. "Look, sis! You're on the news."

"I know." Kate struggled up to a sitting position.

"You're famous."

"Hardly. Anyway, everyone will be looking at him, not me."

"That sick bastard." Courtney looked towards the floor, her hair falling forward to hide her face. Kate knew she was thinking about Peter Buckley. Had *he* been arrested yet? She hoped so. Anderton had expressly forbidden her to be a part of that team. Kate had capitulated without protest, knowing she wouldn't be able to trust herself with either Peter Buckley or her mother.

As if summoned by thought, Kate's mobile rang and the name Mary Redman flashed up on the screen. Caught unawares, Kate had time to think *why don't I have her number saved as 'Mum?'* She pressed the button to take the call before she could come up with the answer.

"You bitch, Kelly!"

From years of experience, Kate could usually gauge her mother's precise level of drunkenness simply by the slur in her voice. This time, Mary's inebriation was harder to place, though, given the fury that was emanating from the receiver.

"Mum—"

"Don't fucking 'mum' me! I bet you were just waiting for the chance to ruin things for me, weren't you? It's those coppers who have ruined you, you think the worst of everyone, you can't even treat your own mother with a bit of respect—"

Courtney was looking at her, wide-eyed. Kate tried to smile reassuringly through the battering of her right ear drum.

"Mum—"

"You're a liability, Kelly, you never had no respect for me, ever—"

"You're drunk," said Kate. She said it coldly, trying to keep a lid on her own anger.

"So what if I fucking am? You're driving me to it."

"I want to talk to you when you're sober."

"I know why you did this," said Mary, half sobbing. Kate heard the smash of a glass on the other end of the line and winced. "You're jealous. Jealous of me."

Kate laughed mirthlessly. She could feel her hold on her temper gradually slipping, like an oiled bottle through slick fingers.

"Yeah, right, Mum. I'm jealous."

"Too right you are. Perhaps if you got yourself a man, you wouldn't go around trying to ruin everyone's else's. Eh? Eh, Kelly? Tell me I'm wrong. Tell me I'm wrong! Tell me—"

Kate pressed the 'end call' button as viciously as she could. Then she threw the phone down hard on the sofa and fought the urge to punch the cushion next to her while screaming out her rage. Instead, she dropped her head into her hands, breathing raggedly. After a moment, she felt the timid touch of Courtney's hand on her trembling shoulder.

"Sis?" Courtney whispered.

Kate sat up and smoothed her hair back, breathing deeply.

"It's all right," she began. "Listen, Courtney—"

The doorbell interrupted her.

"Who's that?" Courtney said, getting up and moving towards the door.

"Wait." Kate put a hand out to stop her. She had a horrible feeling it might be press, although that might just be paranoia from watching herself on the news. She peeked cautiously out from behind the living room curtains. It was a man on the doorstep but who it was, she couldn't quite make out...in that moment, the figure turned, and she realised it was Jay.

"Are you okay? Are you okay?" was all that she could say, moments later, as she stood with her arms around him on the doorstep, the two of them swaying slightly. The police had let him go. She tightened her arms around him for a moment, squeezing him so he cried out in mock protest.

Kate released him. By now, Courtney had come into the hallway. She shrieked and flung herself at her brother.

"Jesus," he gasped, staggering backwards. "I'm all right. Let me sit down, at least."

The two girls half dragged him into the living room and pushed him down onto the sofa.

"They let you go," said Courtney, still hugging him.

Jay smiled up at Kate. He had a strange kind of euphoria about him—a shaky sort of smile pinned to his face. He put one arm around Courtney and leant back, sighing out what sounded like a long-pent-up breath.

Kate sat down on the other chair. She was so relieved she was almost shaking. If they'd released him, then that meant...

"What happened, Jay?"

"Can I have a drink first?"

Kate got him a glass of wine, the last of the bottle that Olbeck had brought with him on the night they'd first seen Nathan Vertz on the small screen. Jay tossed it back in three mouthfuls.

"I needed that," he said with a gasp in his voice.

"What *happened*?"

"I changed my statement."

"They didn't charge you?"

"*Charge* me? Of course not. Charge me with what? I got a caution, that's all."

"A caution..." Kate got up and began pacing around the room. Then she came and sat down again.

"Tell me—tell us about it."

Jay put a hand to his forehead for a second, rubbing his temple.

"It was all over the papers...about Nathan Vertz, I mean. How he was under arrest for Elodie's murder." Kate nodded, listening intently. "Well, sis, that's when I knew I had to do something. I knew he couldn't have killed her."

"How did you know?" whispered Kate. Despite the fact he'd been released, despite the fact he was her brother, a tiny part of her was dreading hearing him say the words *because I killed her*.

But of course, he hadn't. Jay confirmed that with his next sentence.

"I knew he couldn't have killed her because he was with me most of the night. We were definitely together during the time of the murder."

"With you?"

"Yeah." For the first time, Jay dropped his gaze.

"Right," said Kate. "Clearly you mean—what do you mean? What were you doing?"

Jay had a small, sheepish smile on his lips.

"Massive amounts of charlie, sis. I'm sorry."

"Charlie? Cocaine? Oh Jay—" Kate checked herself, the first exclamation of anger choked down. Now was not the time for a lecture on the perils of drugs. "All right, I'm not thrilled to hear that. But we'll get to that later. You and Nathan were together on the night Elodie died?"

"Yeah. Most of the night, actually. You know how it is—" Now it was Jay's turn to check himself. "All right, so you don't know how it is. Anyway—I knew he wasn't anywhere near Elodie for most of the night. Tom vouched for him too."

"Tom?"

"Lorelei's singer. He wasn't with us all night—he just bought some weed off Nathan and went home—but he was there for some of it."

Kate sighed and sat back against the back of the sofa. She looked at her brother with a mixture of pride, anger and exasperation.

"Why now, Jay?" she asked. "Why come clean now? When I think of all that time I spent trying to persuade you to even give a bloody statement... Why on Earth didn't you mention this when they arrested you, for God's sake?"

Jay rolled his eyes. "Why d'you think? I didn't fancy getting banged up in the slammer for doing Class A's, did I? I knew they had no evidence that showed I had anything to do with Elodie being killed. I mean, I know that because I didn't do it. I was *going* to mention it if I thought they wouldn't let me go. Tom would have backed me up if he had to, just like he did for Nathan."

"So you put yourself back in danger of arrest to clear Nathan Vertz's name?" said Kate, slowly. "Why? He's not your friend. I didn't even know you knew him."

"I barely do know him. That wasn't why I did it." Jay looked Kate directly in the eyes, as if to give extra weight to his next few words. "I did it for Elodie."

"Elodie—"

Jay nodded. "I did it for Elodie. She loved Nathan. I mean, she really loved him. I didn't like him, I didn't like him giving her drugs, but it was her decision, after all. He didn't push her into it. She loved him, and he loved her."

"But what about you?" Kate leant forward and put her hand on Jay's arm. "You loved her too, didn't you?"

Jay had a strange expression on his face, half smile, half grimace. He shook his head.

"I liked her," he said slowly. "I fancied her. I thought sometimes I *did* love her, or that I was in love with her, whatever you want to call it. But there was something that put me off. Elodie was hard work. She wasn't...there was something wrong with her. Something damaged. Christ knows I've had enough practice at spotting that. Know what I mean, sis? Eh, Courtney?"

His two sisters didn't agree or contradict him. They were all at that moment thinking of their mother and their chaotic childhood, the childhood that they seemed to have come through in one piece, if only just.

Kate glanced at her mobile phone, half hidden

beneath a cushion. *You bitch, Kelly*. What kind of mother said that to her own child?

Jay went on. "I guess I just knew, somehow, that I had to leave her well alone. I knew she'd be bad for me."

Kate opened her mouth to speak, but he hadn't finished.

"Maybe I should have, though," he said quietly. "Maybe I should have. I don't know. Right now, I'm feeling like I—I let her down. That I should have tried harder to help her. That's why I had to do what I just did. Because I feel like I let Elodie down, and I should have done more to help her. This is the only thing I could do."

His voice broke and he put a hand up to his eyes. Courtney put an arm around him from where she was sitting next to him on the sofa and laid her cheek against his shuddering back.

Kate sat back, easing the ache in her shoulders.

"What about you, Courtney?" she asked, feeling as if she may as well uncover all the dark secrets at once. "What were you trying to tell me the other day? Was it about Jay? Or was it…" She stopped and swallowed. "Was it about Peter?"

Courtney didn't blush. Instead her features seemed to shrink a little, pulling together as if something were tightening inside her. Kate saw, and her heart sank.

"Oh Christ," she said. "Did he do something to you? What did he do?"

Courtney shook her head violently, and Kate remembered to breathe again.

"Not me," she said. "He never laid a finger on me. I saw him taking photos of Jade."

Kate's lungs locked up again. "Photos? What kind of photos?"

Courtney shook her head again, her big, dark eyes wide.

"Not *those* kind. Just pictures on his phone. But I just—I didn't like it. I thought it was weird. 'Cos Jade didn't know he was taking them. I didn't know who to tell, what to do or nothing."

Kate pressed her trembling hands together. She thought of her little sister, fourteen years old, and Peter Buckley lurking behind doors and windows with his phone, snapping away. If she saw that man again, she would kill him and sod her job. She took a deep breath.

"Did you tell Mum?"

Jay half laughed. Courtney, looking miserable, nodded. "What did she say?"

"She just went crazy mad. Shouted a lot and told me I was wrong."

Kate sat silently, almost felled again by another wave of anger, this time against her mother. How could Mary be so blind, so unreasonable; how *could* she? To think of poor Courtney, trying to do the best she could for her baby sister, verbally and possibly physically abused by the one person who was supposed to keep her daughters safe... For a moment, she found herself reaching for her mobile, determined to have it out with her mother, before sanity prevailed and she sat back against the cushions of the sofa, clenching her teeth with suppressed rage.

She pulled herself together. Courtney and Jay were looking at her anxiously. She sat up straight and tried to smile reassuringly at them. She wasn't a mother (*not a* real *one at least*, that hateful little voice whispered) but with these two, she felt like more than a big sister. They were her responsibility. They had to be, because who else was going to look after them?

"All right," she said eventually. "Try not to worry, Courts. I won't let anything happen to Jade. I promise you."

Later, when both Jay and Courtney were asleep, Kate sat up in her own bed with her laptop warming her legs under the covers. She brought up the internet browser and typed Nathan Vertz's name into the search box. Patiently, she followed each link, reading about the Butterkins films, interviews with Nathan as a boy, his Wikipedia page again. At one point, she got up and made herself a strong coffee, shivering in the cold kitchen as the kettle boiled. Back at the computer, she dug down into the third and fourth page of links, forcing her eyelids to remain open. Why was she doing this? What was she hoping to achieve? She asked herself this, several times, but still she kept reading.

A name caught her eye in the metadata of one of the links to Vertz's name—the name of a now-notorious television presenter of the seventies and eighties. Curious, Kate clicked on the link, which brought her through to a newspaper article reporting on the out-of-court settlement by the presenter to the family of Nathan Vertz. She rubbed her tired eyes and read on, several phrases leaping out at her. *Sexual abuse of a minor...civil case... payment of thousands...several other cases due to come to court...* Kate thought for a moment, biting her lip. So Nathan Vertz had suffered sexual abuse as a little boy? Or had accused someone of abusing him, at least?

She read through the reportage again. What kind of parents accept an out-of-court settlement for something so serious? She leant back against the headboard and closed her eyes. No wonder Vertz was depressed.

She could feel herself falling backwards into sleep. Yawning, she closed the laptop, put it on the floor next to her bed and lay down, pulling the duvet cover up to her chin.

# Chapter Twenty

THE WATER OF THE RIVER was green, translucent, dappled with sunlight. It was not cold, but as warm as a bath, as warm as the waters of the tropics. Kate swam easily through the waterweeds, which tangled and tugged at her arms and legs. Brightly-coloured fish wound in and out of the water plants, the kind of fish never seen in a British river but only in the land of dreams; their appearance caused Kate no surprise.

As she swam, she became aware of someone beside her and turned. It was Elodie, dead Elodie, the bones of her skull showing beneath the bleached skin of her face. Kate felt no fear; she was glad to see her. The two women swam side by side through the wavering, pellucid water. Then Elodie reached out for Kate, the hard bones of her skeletal hand winding around Kate's living fingers. She was pulling Kate through the water, up, urging her on, up, up...until Kate's face broke through the surface of the river into the dazzle of light beyond...

Kate woke then, her eyes clicking open just as if someone had thrown a switch in her brain. She stared up at the barely visible ceiling, looking blankly through the early morning darkness. She could still feel the touch of Elodie's hand in hers, a fading ghost-memory. Then she sighed out loud. The pieces were falling into place, click, click, click... there were no fireworks this time, no bright flare of comprehension: just a gradual clearing of the fog, the surface of the river becoming transparent so the hidden, drowned things beneath became visible.

It was six o'clock in the morning; too early to call. Kate got up, showered, dressed and breakfasted, moving quietly so as not to wake the others but jittery with impatience. At quarter to seven, she picked up the phone.

Anderton answered on the third ring. He sounded as wide awake as she was—perhaps he was an early riser. Or perhaps he'd been waiting for her to call.

He didn't say much but listened intently.

"Where's the evidence?" was all he said after Kate finished speaking.

"I need to talk to Sam. It'll be there, I'm sure of it."

"You're probably right. Meet me at the office and pick up Mark along the way."

Before she left, Kate checked on her siblings.

Courtney was buried beneath a bunched duvet, one bare foot poking out the side of the bed. Kate gently covered it up again. Jay was crashed on the sofa, one hand beneath his cheek once again. Kate left them a brief note, scrawled two kisses on the end of it and put on her jacket, winding a scarf tightly about her neck. It was bitterly cold, the sky a leaden grey, a promise of snow in the icy air. She closed the front door almost noiselessly behind her.

She and Olbeck didn't speak much on the way to the office. She'd explained her theory, and he'd sat silently for a few minutes, his quick mind processing what she'd said.

"Don't say anything yet," Kate said, seeing he was preparing to speak. "Let's just see what we've got before we go any further."

"Okay."

They went straight to the IT room, which was bustling with activity. Sam was hunched over one of the impounded laptops, clicking the mouse with bleary determination. He looked up as Kate and Olbeck approached. His round face was pallid with exhaustion, dark circles under his eyes echoing the curve of his glasses.

Kate explained what they wanted as quickly and succinctly as she could. Sam nodded.

"I'll bring it up."

Anderton was already in his office, pacing back and forth. Kate and Olbeck had only just settled themselves when Sam bustled through the doorway with a bundle of papers in his arms.

"Is this everything?" asked Kate.

Sam shook his head. "Not quite. It's everything we could pull from the first two school iPads, Peter Buckley's laptop and Graham Lightbody's home computer. We're still working on the others."

"That's fine," said Anderton, crisply. "Well done, Sam. Excellent work." Sam smiled tiredly and straightened up a little. "Keep at it and let us have it when you do."

He waited until the door closed. Then Anderton spread the sheets out across his desk.

"Cross check against this list," he said. "We may as well see what we're dealing with here at the same time."

The room filled with the busy feel of intense concentration. Looking at the sheets of paper in her hand, Kate could clearly see the email trails between Peter Buckley and Graham Lightbody's many email accounts. Swapping passwords for closed forums, sending links to protected sites. How long had the two of them known each other? How had they met? The name Alice cropped up several times. A victim of their sick fantasies? An abused child? Kate could feel her mouth turning down. Then she realised. Alice, as in *Alice in Wonderland*. Kate remembered reading about the real-life Alice in a magazine article, recalled the rumours and innuendo that circled around the relationship between Lewis Carroll and his seven-year-old muse, Alice Liddell. Kate could recall them now; those weird, provocative photographs of the little girl who'd inspired the classic, taken by the writer of the book. She shuddered.

It was Olbeck who found what they were looking for. Kate and Anderton noticed it seconds after he did. There was a moment of breathless hush. Olbeck put one finger out, gently, touching it to the name they were looking for. He looked up at the other two.

"Of course," Anderton said, softly. "The spider at the centre of the whole rotten web."

They made their way to Anderton's car. As they passed the door that led to the cells, Kate remembered Vertz and asked about him.

"Released on bail," said Anderton, stepping quickly from stair to stair. "He'll be up for possession, intent to supply and a few other things I can think to throw at him, but we couldn't hold him on the murder charge."

"No, I know," said Kate. "So, he's free then?"

Anderton had reached the car. He held the back door open for her, courteously.

"For now," he said. "Why? What's the problem?"

Kate hesitated. Until that moment, she hadn't thought that there was a problem. Now, she was conscious of a faint, creeping sense of unease.

"Nothing," she said, after a second's thought.

She ducked into the car and clipped on her belt. "There's no problem."

"He *was* assessed by the Psych Team," said Anderton, starting the car. "They clearly didn't think he was too much of a risk to himself."

"Yes, I know." Kate saw Olbeck turning round in his seat to catch her eye. He didn't have to say anything—one glance was enough. "It doesn't matter."

Olbeck turned back in his seat to face the front. Anderton glanced at him and caught Kate's eye in the mirror. He didn't say anything, but he pushed down on the accelerator with just a little more pressure.

They didn't say anything else for the duration of the drive. At one point, they passed the river, sparkling in the weak winter sunshine. How cold it must have been for Mike Deedham, jumping in to save Elodie, who was then far beyond saving. When could she have been saved? Why hadn't anyone helped her, when it hadn't been too late?

Kate found she had her eyes shut. She opened them to see the car pulling into the driveway of their destination. The trees were bare, skeletal now: rustling heaps of dead leaves piled against the banks. Anderton was slowing the car. Kate stared at the house before them, willing it to look normal, untouched, unchanged from when she'd last seen it. She spotted the half-open door straight away, but what with the noise of the car and the crunch of its wheels over the gravel, the three officers didn't hear the screaming until the engine was switched off.

They were out of the car in seconds and running towards the open door, Anderton in the lead. He kicked the partly open door open and as they stampeded into the hallway, the screaming became much louder, as if they'd been listening to it underwater and had just cleared the surface. Kate saw a bloodied hand print on the cream paint of the hallway wall, smeared but still recognisable. Drips of blood made a gory trail along the corridor. Then they were in the room with the screaming woman.

Genevieve Duncan was crouched in a foetal position in the armchair where Kate had seen her sitting before, where she'd pulled and picked at the arms. She had her hands up to her face in a characteristic gesture, her open mouth a black, vibrating hole beneath her clenched fingers. The body of Mr Duncan lay on the living room carpet. Because of the pattern of the carpet, the blood stains surrounding him were not immediately obvious, but when Kate saw the damage done to his head and face, she felt like screaming herself.

They found Nathan Vertz in the garden, sitting slackly on the steps that led down to the lawn. He was staring into space, his bloodstained hands hanging loosely at his sides. He didn't try to run or evade arrest. Kate had the impression, as Anderton cautioned him and Olbeck snapped the cuffs around his spattered wrists, that he was somewhere far away, a refugee in a distant land, hiding inside an inner landscape where, perhaps, he'd found some measure of blank and noiseless peace.

# Chapter Twenty One

THE WOMAN IN FRONT OF them sat tensely, sometimes clasping her hands together in front of her, sometimes holding each elbow, hugging her body protectively. Her face, the template for Elodie's golden looks, was rigid; the jawline was sharp, the cheekbones showing bluishly through the skin. Kate wondered whether Genevieve Duncan ever relaxed, if she ever sat in a loose, unstructured way. Well, even if she had once, she would probably never do so again.

As reserved as the woman's posture was, the same could not be said of her voice. She was talking in an endless, brittle monotone, floods of words— all the words, Kate sensed, that she had wanted to say for years but could, or would, not.

"It was always about *her*," said Mrs Duncan. Her hands pressed together once more. "I was always second-best, always. Even with my first husband, Elodie's father... The way he used to fawn over her was just sickening. After she was born, he barely gave me a second glance. Perhaps that would have changed, I don't know... He killed himself, you know, oh, not deliberately, but he drank too much and smashed himself up in his car. Elodie was only five. It was difficult, just the two of us. Two *females* in one house. That was something my mother always said to me: a house isn't big enough for two women, and she certainly made sure that was true in ours—"

Kate sat opposite from her, keeping as neutral a face as she could. Anderton and Olbeck were also in the room, sat slightly back from the table. The duty solicitor, a care-worn, grey-haired woman in her fifties sat next to Genevieve.

"Then I met Tom. I thought he was the answer to my prayers, a nice, handsome, well-off man willing to take on another man's daughter. I was so happy when he proposed." Mrs Duncan gave a laugh that was half sob. "And it was all to do with Elodie. She was all he wanted. Do you know what it's like to have your husband reject you for your own daughter? Do you have any comprehension of how humiliating that was? It was never about me. It was all about *her*."

Kate could see Olbeck struggle not to show the distaste this woman's self-pitying rant was engendering. She had no such qualms herself.

"Your husband was sexually abusing your daughter, Mrs Duncan," she said, making no attempt to hide the disgust in her voice. She wondered whether Anderton would pull her up. He remained silent.

Mrs Duncan looked at her with scorn.

"She encouraged him," she said, and this time, Olbeck did make a sound, a smothered exclamation of outrage. "She must have encouraged him."

"She was *eight years old* when they met," said Kate. "How can you say that?"

Mrs Duncan seemed not to hear her. She was staring at her hands knotted together on her lap, at the wedding ring on her finger that gleamed under the harsh strip lights.

"He used to read her bedtime stories," she said, *apropos* of nothing. Kate remembered the childish books by Elodie's bed and inwardly shuddered. Was that when the abuse had started? Was Elodie's bedroom so far away from her parents' room because she was trying to get away—or was it that her stepfather had given her that room to be sure of not being overheard?

"Did you daughter tell you she was being abused?" Kate asked. "Did she *try* to tell you? Did she ask you for help?" She could feel her own hands clenching into fists under cover of the table. She remembered her own mother's reaction to Courtney's plea. "Did you even listen? Or did you tell her she was making it all up?"

"Kate..." said Anderton, and Kate subsided, choking down her anger.

There was silence for a moment. Genevieve Duncan continued to regard her hands as if they fascinated her. Perhaps, thought Kate, they did, considering what they had done.

Anderton spoke quietly.

"Here's what I think happened on that night, Mrs Duncan. Perhaps you'll tell me if I'm right or wrong."

Mrs Duncan gave no indication that she'd heard him. Anderton pressed on regardless. "Elodie got home late that night. She'd quarrelled with Vertz, nothing major, just the normal kind of lovers' tiff that happens now and again. Perhaps that's why she didn't go home with him. If only she had, she might still be alive."

Kate was watching Genevieve Duncan's face keenly. At Anderton's last remark, it contracted very slightly, a bare flicker of the muscles that was quickly controlled. How tightly had this woman kept her emotions over the years? Kate thought of a spring, wound tighter and tighter...until one day, it snaps.

Anderton went on speaking.

"Your husband went to her room, as he was wont to do. Was it every night, Genevieve? Did he ever leave her alone?"

Mrs Duncan said nothing, but a tide of red suffused her face. Was it embarrassment—or fury?

"I think you heard him leave your bed," said

203

Anderton, watching her closely. "You followed him up to Elodie's room. I don't think it was what you saw that compelled you to act. After all, I don't believe for one second you didn't know your daughter was being abused, night after night. No, that wasn't what made you snap. That wasn't what made you do it."

He stopped speaking for a moment. Some sort of titanic struggle was going on under the skin of Genevieve Duncan's face; years of suppression and denial were being beaten back by the tides of anger.

Anderton spoke again.

"The baby," he said softly, and Mrs Duncan made some sort of noise, a half-choked cry, as if she'd just been struck.

"The baby," repeated Anderton, relentlessly. "You heard Elodie tell her stepfather she was pregnant. You immediately jumped to the conclusion that it was your husband's baby. And that was the tipping point."

"She *said* it was his," gasped Genevieve Duncan. "She told him! She was evil, she was sick...it would have been an abomination..."

"Elodie was wrong," said Anderton. "It was Vertz's baby."

Mrs Duncan was shaking. She looked at Anderton through reddened eyes.

"You killed your daughter," said Anderton, in a deceptively gentle voice. "You and your husband, aghast at what you'd done, realised that you couldn't confess. The scandal would be catastrophic, especially for you, who'd spent so many years in denial of the reality of your family's situation. How could you be brave enough to own up to what you'd done? That admitting your actions would mean everything coming out in the open, everyone knowing the grim truth. What did you do with Vertz's letters to Elodie, Genevieve? Did you burn them?" He paused for breath. "Was it because you couldn't bear to see yet another man loving your daughter? The daughter who, in your eyes, had taken all the love that was meant for you?"

Kate was watching Genevieve's face closely. She could see the change of expression, the eyes filming over a little, the metaphorical shutters coming down. The habit of denial was just too strong.

"I don't know what you're talking about," she said in a choked voice. "I think you want to drive me mad."

"Why put her body in the river, Genevieve? Why do that?"

The woman opposite was silent. Then she laughed a laugh that was not quite sane.

"Ophelia," was all she said.

Kate went cold. She realised that Jay's painting *had* been involved, yet not in the way she'd thought. Had Elodie showed her parents the painting? Had they wanted to incriminate Jay, to find a credible suspect? She actually shuddered. Then she realised that it was more than that. Elodie wasn't Ophelia, was she? Ophelia was sat in this interview room, clasping her hands together: a woman driven mad by the cruelty of a man who couldn't, who wouldn't love her.

There was a long moment of silence.

Genevieve Duncan sat up a little straighter. She seemed to gain a little bit of control over herself.

"I wasn't in my right mind that night," she said. She looked Anderton full in the face. "No, that was it. She'd driven me mad by her behaviour. She wasn't—she was so—sick, so *damaged*. It was a kindness. I wasn't in my right mind. No, I wasn't in my right mind."

That was the last thing she said. She withdrew into herself then, staring at her hands, twisting her wedding ring about her thin finger. Nothing that Anderton or Kate or Olbeck could say shook her into talking again. After twenty fruitless minutes, they gave up and Anderton rang for an officer to escort her to the cells.

There was silence for a moment after Mrs Duncan was taken away. Then Anderton sprang up from his chair.

"Come on," he said. "Debrief time."

When they were all gathered in the incident room, Anderton took up his usual position, pacing back and forth before the whiteboards. He had something in his hand, some thin slip of paper. As he reached Elodie's school photograph, he took what was in his hand and pinned it up on the board next to Elodie's image. It was a photograph of Nathan Vertz as a little boy. Kate recognised it as a publicity shot from the first Butterkins film.

Anderton tapped each photograph.

"Two children," he said. "Two abused children. That was their connection, that's what underpinned their relationship. Do you remember what Vertz said? Anyone?"

Olbeck raised his hand. "He said, 'She knew what it was like.' Something like that, anyway."

Anderton nodded.

"Nathan Vertz entered show business at any extremely young age. He was a little boy, vulnerable and unprotected. I'm sure I don't need to remind you that predators can be found in any sphere—anywhere where children can be found."

Kate nodded, thinking of the crisis currently engulfing the BBC. Vertz had named his abuser, but had the accused been the only one to hurt him? She thought of a little blonde boy, a vulnerable child, the parents who should have protected him too interested in chasing fame and fortune to defend their son. She felt a little sick.

"Vertz and Elodie were drawn towards each other, as damaged people so often are. Vertz was a drug dealer, and Elodie was a drug user, so it could be that their relationship was pragmatic, one of convenience—but I'm not convinced. I think they had a genuine love affair. I think they loved each other as fully as two people who'd never been shown any real love could."

Kate remembered Jay saying much the same thing the other night. For a moment, she gave thanks. No matter what her mother's failings had been, at least Kate had always had someone to love. She'd had people to love her back—her brother and sisters.

Anderton was still speaking.

"Thomas Duncan met Genevieve and Elodie when Elodie was eight years old, as we know. Hideous as it is to contemplate, it's quite probable that he married the mother to enable him to abuse her daughter. He certainly wouldn't be the first paedophile to actively target a single mother to gain her trust and have unfettered access to her children."

Kate thought of her own mother, of Jade and Peter Buckley, and felt sick again. At least she had the satisfaction of knowing he would almost certainly be going to prison, although she hated the idea of her sisters having to give evidence at his trial.

"As you also know, the scale and extent of the abuse at Rawlwood College is still being uncovered.

We have several teachers, as well as the headmaster himself, who regularly groomed and abused the children in their care. They targeted the vulnerable ones, the ones who wouldn't speak out."

He pinned a third photograph up on the board, one of a girl with frizzy brown hair. Placed side by side, you could see the resemblance in all three photographs, something in the eyes. A hunted, anxious expression. Kate had seen it, momentarily, at Rawlwood College, before being distracted. It was impossible to see their haunted young faces without tears coming to your eyes.

"Violet Sammidge," said Anderton. He placed a tender finger on her photographed face. "She was one of Graham Lightbody's victims. Possibly one of Duncan's too. She was a young girl, deeply affected by her parents' divorce. An easy target." For a moment, anger vibrated in his voice.

Jane raised her hand.

"You don't think she was murdered too, guv?"

Anderton shook his head. "No, not at all. It was a clear case of suicide. Although..." He paused for a moment, rubbing his chin. "Although you could say she was driven to it by the dreadful actions of Lightbody. So in a sense, he is responsible for her death. Unfortunately, we can't pin that on him."

"He'll get his punishment," said Olbeck, grimly.

"Let's hope so."

Anderton resumed his pacing.

"On the night of the murder, we know Elodie went home after the gig at the Black Horse. We know that her stepfather went up to her room." Kate could see the disgust on her own face mirrored in those of her colleagues. Anderton looked at her. "We have Kate to thank for highlighting the abuse."

Kate shrugged. "Once I'd realised, it just seemed so obvious. But I was wrong as well. I thought her stepfather had killed her."

Anderton tousled his hair and let his hand drop.

"No, Genevieve was the person who strangled Elodie. It's a horrible thought, a mother killing a daughter, but that's what happened. I don't think we'd have to dig too deeply into Genevieve's background to find another story of abuse in *her* childhood. Not that that's any excuse for what she did."

Kate waited until he paused and asked her question. "So Duncan knew Genevieve had killed Elodie?"

"Knew? He almost certainly witnessed it. Why didn't he stop her? Was it because he too thought he was the father of his stepdaughter's baby? Was he in shock? Who knows? He can't tell us."

"Did Nathan Vertz think Thomas Duncan had killed Elodie?" asked Olbeck.

Anderton nodded. "I think so. It tipped him over the edge. He knew about the abuse, of course, but it was the revelation of the baby that drove him to kill. Perhaps all the rage and shame and anger at the abuse he'd suffered in childhood came flooding out. Thomas Duncan became the symbol for what had happened to him as a little boy."

"Poor man," said Kate.

"Yes," said Anderton briefly. "So we have the Duncans colluding to dispose of Elodie's body. You know, Kate, I think they *did* put her body in the river in the hope it would incriminate your brother."

"It nearly did," said Kate, remembering Anderton's rage at her seeming deception. Their eyes met for a moment, and she felt another surge of the attraction that she thought she'd nearly succeeded in tamping down. Did he feel it too? She dropped her gaze, willing herself not to blush.

Anderton cleared his throat.

"A sad case," he said. He turned to the whiteboard and touched the picture of each child gently, just once. "A very sad case. Thank you all for bringing it to the only possible conclusion."

LATER THAT AFTERNOON, KATE SIGNED the last report, capped her pen and pushed her chair away from her desk. She looked over at Olbeck.

"I'm done for the day."

"Good for you. I've still got loads to do."

"Leave it for now, Mark. I'm going for a drive. Why don't you come with me?"

CELINA GRACE

Olbeck considered. Then he stood up and took his coat from the back of his chair.

As they walked towards Kate's car, his phone chimed as a text message came through. "Another new date?" asked Kate, trying to keep the disapproval from her voice as they got into her car.

"Same one, actually," said Olbeck, clipping on his belt. "It'll be our third date."

"Oh, right," said Kate, eyebrows raised. She turned on the engine. "Is it serious?"

Olbeck scoffed. Then he reconsidered.

"Don't know, actually," he said, sounding surprised. "It might be. I like him."

"Good."

Olbeck smiled slyly.

"What about you?"

"What do you mean, 'what about me?'"

"When are we going to get you fixed up?"

"Oh, Mark." For a moment, Anderton's face came into Kate's mind. She dismissed the jump in her lower belly. "I'm all right on my own."

"Sure?"

"Sure," said Kate, trying to sound firm.

They found a parking space not too far away and got out. It was one of those beautiful winter days with pale sunlight and high, wispy white clouds, the leafless trees like living sculptures. Kate and Olbeck walked along beside the river, their feet scuffing over frost-hardened ridges of mud. As they got closer, Kate could see all the flowers, laid out like a colourful carpet along the riverbank. She and Olbeck stopped a little way away and regarded the heaped blooms. She thought again of the painting with Elodie on the riverbank, pale and blue-lipped, entwined with flowers.

Something caught her eye, a tiny gleam of pale yellow, right at the water's edge. She looked harder and then nudged Olbeck.

"Look."

Olbeck followed her pointing finger past all the gaudy, plastic-wrapped hothouse flowers to the little blossom growing through the frozen mud.

"A primrose?" he said. "Growing in November?"

"Yes."

"That's weird. It's been so cold, you wouldn't have thought it would live."

They regarded the flower for a moment, its delicate yellow petals trembling in the cold wind.

"It's for Elodie," said Kate softly.

Olbeck looked at her quizzically. "It's not like you to be sentimental."

Kate thought of something else Jay had said, that Vertz had said, that even her stepfather had said.

"Elodie was different," she said.

Olbeck was silent. Kate took one last look at the primrose and turned away.

"Come on, time to go home."

They walked back along the riverbank, quietly, shielding their eyes against the sunlight that gleamed from the surface of the glittering river.

# THE END

# WANT MORE CELINA GRACE?

DID YOU ENJOY THIS BOOK? An honest review left on Amazon, Goodreads, Shelfari or LibraryThing is *always* welcome, and really important for indie authors! The more reviews an indie book gets, the easier it is to promote and reach new readers.

Please post a review at Amazon UK or Amazon US.

You can read more from Celina Grace at her blog on writing and self-publishing: http://www.celinagrace.com. Be the first to be informed of promotions, giveaways, new releases and subscriber-only benefits by subscribing to her (occasional) newsletter. You can download a **free** copy of her short story collection **A Blessing From The Obeah Man** by signing up to the newsletter.

http://www.celinagrace.com

**Twitter:**
@celina__grace

**Facebook:**
http://www.facebook.com/authorcelinagrace

Want more Kate Redman? The third novel in the series, **Imago (A Kate Redman Mystery: Book 3)**, is available on Amazon.

# Imago

A Kate Redman Mystery: Book 3

CELINA GRACE

© Celina Grace 2013

# J's Diary

*THE FIRST GIRL'S DEATH WAS an accident.*

I lifted my pen off of the paper and thought for a bit. My pen was poised to cross it out – the impulse trembled up my arm – but in the end, I left the sentence as it was.

I don't really know why I started writing this diary, account, whatever you'd call it. I suppose I wanted a record of what's happened in my life since the first one. Ever since I realised what I had to do to become complete – to unfold into a whole person rather than inhabit the empty shell of one – there's been another urge, almost as strong: the need to write down *why* I do the things I do. I'm not trying to justify anything to anyone, in the unlikely event that someone reads these diaries. The key thing, I suppose, is to be true to myself, to be truthful when I'm talking to myself as I am here, setting down these words. That's the only meaningful thing to do. If I'd only been true to myself from an early age, none of the bad things would have happened. Or maybe they would. Who knows?

So, in the interest of truth, the first death wasn't really an *accident*. I've just checked my dictionary and the definition of "accident" is something like *an unfortunate event that happens unintentionally*. Her death was certainly unfortunate – for her – and it was, at the time, unintentional. I didn't plan it; I didn't spends hours and days fantasising about bringing it about as I have done with the other ones. So you could say it was accidental, I suppose, although I'd have a hard time convincing a jury.

It won't come to that, though. Now I'm getting good at this. It's a new skill, as well as a calling, and I've always been a fast learner. It makes me shiver in anticipation when I think that I could go on like this, year after year, getting better each time. Each time more perfect and more fulfilling than the last one. All those girls out there, for me. None of them have any idea that I am watching and waiting, waiting for the next time...the next death. None of them have any idea because I am in disguise. They don't fear me. Quite the opposite. It makes it twice as fun. Fun. That's certainly a surprising choice of words, especially for me, but that's what it is. It *is* fun – as well as the greatest pleasure I've ever known. Why don't they tell you this? Why do they lie? I feel like I'm the keeper of a secret only a few have discovered.

I know the next time will be soon; I've learnt to recognise the signs. I think I even know who it will be. She's oblivious, of course, just as she should be. All the time, I watch and wait, and she has no idea, none at all. And why would she? I'm disguised as myself, the very best disguise there is.

# Chapter One

KATE RAN.

Her breath rasped in and out of her lungs; her leg muscles burned. A drop of sweat rolled into the corner of her dry mouth. It felt as if she'd been running forever, weaving among the people on the pavements, the shock of her feet hitting the concrete reverberating through her muscles. Every fibre of her being cried out for her to stop, but she couldn't – she was afraid. The man was a sadist, a brutal sadist. She struggled on up a slight incline, her face burning, her lungs crying out for air. At the top of the hill, she had to stop, bent double, gasping for breath. The man following her at an effortless, loping run drew up alongside her.

"Come on, Kate. We've still got two miles to go."

"I can't," gasped Kate, when she had enough oxygen in her lungs to speak. "I'll be sick."

"You won't."

"Will."

The man appeared to relent. "All right. Take a two-minute breather."

Kate staggered over to a convenient bench and fell onto it. She put her roasting face down between her knees.

"Can't – do – this," she said, between gasps.

Detective Sergeant Mark Olbeck sat down beside her and stretched his legs out in front of him.

"It's only a bloody half marathon, for God's sake," he said. "Thirteen miles. It's nothing."

Kate sat back up again, marginally more comfortable, although still breathing hard.

"I'm too – unfit. Someone else will have to – do it."

"You'll *get* fit. That's the whole point of us going out running. Come on, you said you'd do it. It's for charity, remember."

"I can't get fit enough in three weeks."

"Well that's all the time you've got. You've got to be part of the team. If you pull out now, we won't have enough people."

Kate knew this was right. The Abbeyford Charity Half Marathon team from the police station had consisted of Olbeck, Detective Constable Theo Marsh and Detective Constable Ravinder Cheetam until Theo had broken his ankle playing football and had to drop out.

"There's Jerry. And Jane."

"You know as well as I do that Jane's got two

small children and no partner. She can't go out in the evenings at the drop of a hat. And Jerry would probably have a coronary or something if we made him run, the poor old bugger."

Kate leant back against the back of the bench and closed her eyes. She knew all this already, which made her feel even worse about her lack of enthusiasm.

"Don't get comfortable," warned Olbeck. "Come on. On we go."

Kate heaved the deepest sigh her abused lungs could muster. Then she lurched to her feet, and they jogged on through the streets of Abbeyford.

They stopped at the bridge that spanned the river Avon, leaning against the stone parapet and watching the glittering waters slide beneath them. It was a beautiful summer's day, the sky blue but wisped with a filmy curtain of white cloud, the sun gaining in strength by the hour.

"You know, Mark, I'm really not sure I can do this," puffed Kate. She leant her head on her folded arms for a moment and then raised it, looking out at the sparkling water.

"You'll be fine," said Olbeck. "And you'll feel very proud of yourself when you finish."

"I've done plenty of things I'm already proud of," said Kate. "I don't feel that putting one foot in front of the other very quickly qualifies as any kind of great achievement."

Mark grinned. "God, you're narky today."

"It's the unaccustomed blood rushing to my head."

There was a muffled buzzing from Mark's back pocket. He fished his phone out, frowned and answered the call.

"Hello sir. No, we're not doing anything."

Kate waited, knowing it was something serious. She had that familiar feeling she got every time a new case began: tension, anxiety and yes, shamefully, a little bit of excitement, which was tempered with relief – at least she wouldn't have to do any more running that day.

Olbeck said goodbye and put the phone back in his pocket. His partner raised her eyebrows.

"That was Anderton."

"So I gathered. What is it?"

"Dead woman, down by the canal. We've been called in."

"Let's go, then."


Abbeyford was a large market town in the southwest of England. In addition to the river Avon, one of several so named in the country, the town also had a canal running through it. In earlier times, goods had been brought to the town from neighbouring cities, and canal boats pulled by horses moved slowly along the paths by the water to be unloaded at the tiny docks. The canal freight trade had long since gone, and the canal docks in Abbeyford had gradually fallen into disrepair and, eventually, disrepute. The warehouse windows were all broken, the glass in the few remaining panes dulled with dirt and moss. A long-ago fire had gutted one of the buildings, leaving its blackened girders exposed like the charred bones of an animal. Rubbish, dead leaves and dirt were heaped in every corner.

Kate had never been to the area before; she was barely aware of its existence. Perhaps the other Abbeyford residents had a similar knowledge of this part of town, and this was why the killer had chosen to dump the body here. Or had killer and victim met here?

As it turned out, Kate wasn't off the jogging hook after all. She and Olbeck were close enough to the site to make their way there on foot, and Olbeck had insisted that they run, "to get in some more training." Kate arrived at the scene knowing that her face was tomato-red and that her tracksuit was stained with patches of sweat, but after one look at the huddled body of the woman on the ground, these minor concerns faded away.

Scene of Crime officers had already erected the tent that hid the body from prying eyes. Kate and Olbeck ducked under the flap that covered the entrance. The victim was a small, thin woman, with long, dark hair tied tightly back in a high ponytail. She lay on her side, curled in a foetal position, her back to the detectives. One dirty-soled foot was bare; the scuffed silver ballet pump that had fallen from it rested a few inches away. Kate couldn't see any obvious wounds, although the mottled, bare legs were spattered with small amounts of blood.

She studied the scene as intently as she could in the short time that she had, taking in everything that she could see. *Get a feel for the scene*, Anderton was always telling them. *It's amazing what you can pick up without even realising. It can come in very handy as the case progresses.* Kate knew she would never again have this first impression, so she observed with laser-intensity focus, trying to burn the image onto her retinas and into her mind.

Detective Chief Inspector Anderton was there along with Detective Constables Jerry Hindley and Ravinder Cheetam – Rav to his friends and colleagues. The three of them were in a huddle, talking quietly, whilst behind them, the scene was being preserved, photographed and otherwise documented by the Scene of Crime officers. Anderton looked up as Kate and Olbeck approached.

"You got here commendably quickly," was his opening remark. "Glad to see all this running's starting to pay off."

Olbeck gave Kate a 'you *see*?' look but said nothing. He nodded at Jerry and Rav.

"Let's go outside," said Anderton. "Too many people in here."

Outside, the air felt fresh and the sunlight was warm and welcoming on Kate's upturned face.

"What's been happening?" she asked.

"The body was discovered this morning," said Anderton. "A couple of hours ago, so that makes it, what – twelve thirty or so?"

"Who found it?" asked Kate.

"Two young lads. They were a bit reticent about why they were down here in the first place. Probably here to do some tagging or something. They're back at the station at the moment, giving their statements."

"Cause of death?" asked Olbeck.

"We don't yet know. Stanton should be able to tell us more when he's finished – talk of the devil—" Anderton looked up as the white-clad figure of the pathologist emerged from the tent. "Stanton. Stanton!" he called. "What's the quick and dirty?"

Doctor Andrew Stanton joined the group, brightening a little as he realised Kate was amongst them. He had an undisguised admiration for her, which always led to a day's worth of teasing from Olbeck after the three of them met.

"Hi guys. Hi Kate," he added, with special, caressing attention. The other men grinned, and

Kate managed to grit her teeth and smile politely at the same time.

"What have we got?" asked Anderton.

Stanton immediately became professional.

"Stab wounds, several of them, mostly through the lower thoracic region. Stomach and lower chest."

Anderton shook his head.

"Definitely one for us, then. Oh well. Any sign of sexual assault?"

"Difficult to tell. I'll be able to give you a better answer once we've done the PM."

"Right," said Anderton. "Stab wounds. That puts another possible spin on things." He didn't elaborate on what this spin could be. "Any chance of fixing the time of death?"

Stanton shrugged.

"Probably sometime early in the morning, very early. Two or three o'clock. You know I can't be accurate at this stage. You'll have to wait for the PM."

"It gives us a starting point," said Anderton, briefly. "Okay, thanks, Andrew. We'll speak later."

Once Doctor Stanton had left, Anderton ducked into the tent, quickly followed by Rav and Olbeck. Kate found herself standing alone with Jerry Hindley, and her heart sank a little. Jerry was the colleague she knew and liked the least. From the very start of her career at Abbeyford, he'd made it plain that he didn't like her. She'd asked Olbeck and Theo why this might be, and they'd explained that it was probably jealously. "You got the promotion he'd been angling for, Kate," Olbeck had said, and although this sounded plausible, it seemed strange that he'd still be acting hurt and resentful two years later. Again she reminded herself that she didn't care about the opinion of someone so petty and sexist. Occasionally she'd attempt to be friendly, wondering whether he'd ever respond in the same way. She tried again now.

"What do you think happened, Jerry?"

He sighed in an irritated manner. "Didn't you hear the guv? We don't know anything other than what you just heard."

Kate said nothing more. Why did she bother? Was she trying to make him like her? Why? She didn't care about his opinion, did she?

She was relieved to see the other officers exit the tent and make their way back to where she stood.

"Do we have an ID on the victim yet, sir?" Kate asked Anderton, provoking an irritated sigh from Jerry. She ignored him.

Anderton shook his head.

"There's no ID at all on the body. No cards, no purse, no bag."

"Really? That's strange. You'd expect her to have a purse at least, even if she didn't use a handbag."

"Exactly," said Anderton. "It was almost certainly

removed from the body by our perpetrator." He looked at the still surface of the canal. "We're going to have to have that searched. It could easily be in there, as well as the murder weapon."

Olbeck was glancing around at the buildings surrounding them.

"Any cameras here?" he asked. "CCTV footage would help."

"I can't see any," said Kate, scanning the scene. "It doesn't look the sort of place where people would care about vandalism or theft."

"Right, well," said Anderton. "We need to start digging. We don't know whether the murder actually took place here, although from the blood found at the scene, it seems likely. We don't know who the victim is. We don't know what the murder weapon was – yes, some kind of knife, but what kind? We're currently operating from a standpoint of complete ignorance, and that's not a position I like to be in." He paused for breath. "Let's get back to HQ, and we'll take it from there."

Buy Imago (A Kate Redman Mystery: Book 3) on Amazon now.

# Acknowledgements

Many thanks to all the following splendid souls:

Chris Howard for the brilliant cover designs; Brenda Errichiello for proof-reading and editing; lifelong friends and Schlock Monsters David Hall, Ben Robinson and Alberto Lopez; Kathleen and Pat McConnell, Anthony Alcock, Ross McConnell, Naomi White, Mo Argyle, Lee Benjamin, Bonnie Wede, Sherry and Amali Stoute, Cheryl Lucas, Georgia Lucas-Going, Steven Lucas, Loletha Stoute and Harry Lucas, Helen Parfect, Helen Watson, Emily Way, Sandy Hall, Kristýna Vosecká; and of course my ever-loved and loving Chris, Mabel, Jethro and Isaiah.

**This book is for my brother, Ross McConnell, who patiently answers all my questions about police procedures. Thanks, bro. This is for you, with love.**

Printed in Great Britain
by Amazon

51766317R00139